Sabine Baring-Gould

Arminell

A social Romance. Vol. I

Sabine Baring-Gould

Arminell
A social Romance. Vol. I

ISBN/EAN: 9783744780308

Printed in Europe, USA, Canada, Australia, Japan

Cover: Foto ©Andreas Hilbeck / pixelio.de

More available books at **www.hansebooks.com**

A Social Romance

BY THE

AUTHOR OF "MEHALAH," "JOHN HERRING," ETc.

IN THREE VOLUMES

VOL. I.

LONDON:

METHUEN & CO., 18 BURY STREET, W.C.

1890

ARMINELL.

CHAPTER I.

SUNDAY SCHOOL.

SUNDAY-SCHOOL on the ground floor of the keeper's cottage that stood against the church-yard, in a piece nibbled out of holy ground. Some old folks said this cottage had been the church-house where in ancient days the people who came to divine service stayed between morning prayer and evensong, ate their mid-day meal and gave out and received their hebdomadal quotient of gossip. But such days were long over, the house had been used as a keeper's lodge for at least a hundred years. The basement consisted of one low hall exactly six feet one inch from floor to rafters. There was no ceiling between it and the upper house—only a flooring laid on the

A

rafters. In pre-traditional days the men had sat and eaten and drunk in the room above, and the women in that below, between services, and their horses had been stabled where now the keeper had his kennel.

The basement chamber was paved with slabs of slate. Rats infested the lodge, they came after the bones and biscuits left by the dogs. The pheasants' food was kept there, the keeper's wife dropped her dripping, and the children were not scrupulous about finishing their crusts. The rats undermined the slates, making runs beneath the pavement to get at the box of dog biscuits, and the sacks of buckwheat, and the parcels of peppercorns; consequently the slates were not firm to walk on. Moreover, in the floor was a sunless secret cellar, of but eighteen inches in depth, for the reception of liquor, or laces or silks that had not paid the excise. The slates over this place, long disused, were infirm and inclined to let whoever stepped on them down.

During the week the keeper's wife washed in the basement and slopped soapy water about, that ran between the slates and formed puddles, lurking under corners, and when, on Sunday, the incautious foot rested on an angle of slate, the slab tilted and squirted forth the stale unsavoury water.

The room, as already said, was unceiled. The rafters were of solid oak ; the boards above were of deal, and had shrunk in places, and in places dropped out the core of their knots. The keeper's children found a pleasure in poking sticks and fingers through, and in lying flat on the floor with an eye on the knot-hole, surveying through it the proceedings in the Sunday-school below.

About the floor in unsystematic arrangement spraddled forms of deal, rubbed by boys' trousers to a polish. Some of these forms were high in the leg, others short. No two were on a level, and no two were of the same length. They were rudely set about the floor in rhomboidal shapes, or rather in trapeziums, which according to Euclid have no defined shapes at all.

There was a large open fireplace at one end of the room, in which in winter a fire of

wood burned.   When it burned the door had
to be left wide open, because of the smoke,
consequently Sunday-school was held in
winter in a draught.   At the extremity of the
room, opposite the fireplace stood Moses and
Aaron—not in the flesh, nor even in spirit,
but in "counterfeit presentment" as large as
life, rudely painted on board.   They had
originally adorned the east end of the chancel ;
when, however, the fashion of restoring
churches set in, Orleigh Church had been
done up, and Moses and Aaron had been supplanted to make room for a horrible reredos
of glazed tiles.   One of the Sunday-school
scholars, a wag, had scribbled mottoes from
their mouths, on scrolls, and had made Aaron
observe to Moses, " Let us cut off our noses ; "
to which the meekest of men was made to re-
join, " It is the fashion to wear 'em."   But
through orthographical weakness, fashion had
been spelled *fashum*, and wear 'em had been
rendered *warum*.

But why was the Sunday-school held in
the basement of the keeper's cottage ?   For
the best of good reasons.   There was

no other room conveniently near the church in which it could be held.

Lady Lamerton could not live in peace without a Sunday-school. To her, the obligation to keep the ten commandments was second to the obligation to keep Sunday-school. How could the ten commandments be taught, unless there were a Sunday-school in which to teach them ? About a century ago Mr. Raikes invented and introduced this institution ; it spread like measles, schools multiplied like maggots. It became an incumbus on consciences. It was supposed to be the panacea for all moral evil. There are still to be found persons with childlike faith in Sunday-schools, as there are to be found persons who believe in spontaneous combustion and calomel.

The national school was two miles distant, near the village. The church stood in the grounds of Orleigh Park, and its satellite, the Sunday-school, necessarily near it.

In Yorkshire it is customary among the lower classes at dinner, when there is meat, to introduce first a huge and heavy slab of pudding, and the young people are expected to devour a pound's weight of this before meat is put on their plates. It is thought, and justly, that a grounding of leaden dough will make their appetites less keen for roast beef. On the same principle the disciples of Mr. Raikes serve out Sunday-school, slabby and heavy, to young church-folk, before Church worship, to abate in some degree their relish for it.

There had been some difficulty about a habitat for the Sunday-school. Lady Lamerton had tried to hold it in the laundry of the great house, but the children in muddy weather had brought in so much dirt that no laundry-work could be done in the room on Monday till it had been scoured out. Besides—a fearful discovery had been made, better left to the imagination than particularized. Suffice it to say that after this discovery the children were banished the laundry. It must have come from them. From whom else could it have been derived? The laundry-maids were Aphrodites, foam, or rather soap-sud-born, and it could not proceed from such

as they. Some said—but nonsense—there is
no such a thing as spontaneous generation.
Pasteur has exploded that. So all the pupils,
with their prayer-books and Ancient-and-
Moderns under their arms, made an exo-
dus, and went for a while into an outhouse
in the stable-yard. There they did not remain long, for the boys hid behind doors
instead of coming in to lessons, and then
dived into stables to see the horses. One of
them nearly died from drinking embrocation
for spavin, thinking it was cherry-brandy,
and another scratched his ignoble name on the
panel of one of my lord's carriages, with a pin.

So, on the complaint of the coachman, my
lord spoke out, and the Sunday scholars
again tucked their prayer-books and hymnals
under their arms, and, under the guidance of
Lady Lamerton, migrated to a settled habitation in the basement of the keeper's cottage.
The place was hardly commodious, but it had
its advantages—it was near the church.

Lady Lamerton, who presided over the
Sunday-school and collected the Sunday
scholars' club-pence, and distributed that

dreary brown-paper-covered literature that constituted the Sunday-school lending library, was a middle-aged lady with a thin face and very transparent skin, through which every vein showed. There was not much character in her face, but it possessed a certain delicacy and purity that redeemed it from being uninteresting. She was—it could be read in every feature—a scrupulously conscientious woman, a woman strong in doing her duty, and in that only ; one whose head might be and generally was in a profound muddle as to what she believed, but who never for a moment doubted as to what she should do. She would be torn by wild horses rather than not keep Sunday-school, and yet did not know what to teach the children in the school she mustered.

Lady Lamerton, seated on a green garden chair from which the paint was much rubbed away, had about her on three sides of an irregular square the eldest girls of the school. The next class to hers was taken by the Honourable Arminell Inglett, her step-daughter, only child of Lord Lamerton by his first wife.

Miss Inglett was very different in type from her step-mother ; a tall, handsome girl, with dark hair cut short, like a boy's, and eyes of violet blue. She had a skin of the purest olive, no rose whatever in her cheeks, as transparent as Lady Lamerton's, but of a warmer tone, like the mellow of an old painting, whereas that of her step-mother had the freshness and crudeness of a picture from the easel sent to the Royal Academy on the first of May.

Arminell differed from Lady Lamerton in expression as completely as in type of feature and colour. She had an unusual breadth of brow, whereas Lady Lamerton's forehead was narrow. Her eyes had not that patient gentleness that filled the dark blue orbs of her ladyship, they were quick and sparkling. Her lips, somewhat prominent, were full, warm and contemptuous. She held her head erect, with a curl of the mouth, and a contraction of the brows, that expressed impatience at the task on which she was engaged.

On the left side of Miss Inglett sat Captain Tubb, engaged on the illumination of

the souls of the senior boys. Captain Tubb
held no commission in the army or navy, not
even in the volunteers. He was, in fact,
only the manager of a lime-quarry in the
parish, on the estate of Lord Lamerton, but
such heads over gangs of quarry and mining
men bear among the people the courtesy-title
of captain.

Mr. Tubb was a short, pale man with
shiny face much polished, and with sandy
moustache and beard. When he was in perplexity, he put his hand to his mouth, and
stroked his moustache, or his beard under the
chin, turned it up, and nibbled at the ends.

Some folk said that the captain taught in
school so as to stand well with her ladyship,
who would speak a word for him to my lord ;
but the rector thought, more charitably, he
did it for his soul's and conscience sake.
Captain Tubb was a simple man, except in
his business, and in that he was sharp enough.
Perhaps he taught a class from mixed motives, and thought it would help him on a bit
in both worlds.

"Yes," said Lady Lamerton, "yes, Fanny

White, go on. As the list of the canonical
books is known to you all, I require you to
learn the names of these books which, as the
sixth article says, are read for example of life
and instruction of manners; but yet are not
applied to establish any doctrine. After that
we will proceed to learn by heart the names
of the Homilies, twenty-one in all, given in
the thirty-fifth article, which are the more
important, because they are not even read
and hardly any one has a copy of them. Go
on with the uncanonical books. Third Book
of Esdras, Fourth Book of Esdras."

"Tobit," whispered the timid Fanny
White, and curtsied.

"Quite right, Tobit—go on. It is most
important for your soul's health that you
should know what books are not canonical,
and in their sequence. What comes after
Tobit?"

"Judith," faltered Fanny.

"Then a portion of Esther, not found in
Hebrew. What next?"

"Wisdom," shouted the next girl, Polly
Woodley.

"True, but do not be so forward, Polly ; I am asking Fanny White."

"Ecclesiasticks," in a timid, doubtful sigh from Fanny, who raised her eyes to the boards above, detected an eye inspecting her through a knot-hole, laughed, and then turned crimson.

"Not sticks," said Lady Lamerton, sweetly, "you must say—-cus."

A dead silence and great doubt fell on the class.

"Yes, go on—cus."

Then faintly from Fanny, "Please, my lady, mother says I b'aint to swear."

"I don't mind," exclaimed the irrepressible Polly Woodley, starting up, and thrusting her hand forward into Lady Lamerton's face, "Darn it."

Her ladyship fell back in her chair ; the eye was withdrawn from the hole in the floor, and a laugh exploded upstairs.

"I—I didn't mean that," explained the lady, "I meant, not Ecclesiastics, nor Ecclesi-astes, which is canonical, but Ecclesiasti—cus, which is not."

Just then a loud, rolling, grinding sound made itself heard through the school-room, drowning the voices of the teachers and covering the asides of the taught.

"Dear me," said Lady Lamerton, "there is the keeper's wife rocking the cradle again. One of you run upstairs and ask her very kindly to desist. It is impossible for any one to hear what is going on below with that thunder rolling above."

"Please, my lady," said Polly, peeping up through the nearest knot in the superjacent plank, "it b'aint Mrs. Crooks, it be Bessie as is rocking of the baby. Wicked creetur not to be at school."

"It does not matter who rocks the cradle," said her ladyship, "nor are we justified in judging others. One of you—not all at once —you, Polly Woodley, ask Bessie to leave the cradle alone till later."

The whole school listened breathlessly as the girl went out, tramped up the outside slate steps to the floor occupied by the keeper's family above, and heard her say :—

"Now then, Bessie ! What be you

a-making that racket for? My lady says she'll pull your nose unless you stop at once. My lady's doing her best to teach us to cuss downstairs, and her can't hear her own voice wi'out screeching like a magpie."

Then up rose Lady Lamerton in great agitation.

"That girl is intolerable. She shall not have a ticket for good conduct to-day. I will go—no, you run, Joan Ball, and make her return. I will have a proper school-room built. This shall not occur again."

Then Captain Tubb rose to his full height, stood on a stool, put his mouth to the orifice in the plank, placed his hands about his mouth and roared through the hole: "Her ladyship saith Come down."

Presently with unabashed self-satisfaction Polly Woodley reappeared.

"When I send you on an errand," said Lady Lamerton severely, "deliver it as given. I am much displeased."

"Yes, my lady, thank you," answered Polly with cheerful face, and resumed her seat in class.

"Now boys," said Captain Tubb to his class, which was composed of the senior male scholars, including Tom Metters, the rascal who had put the inscriptions in the mouths of Moses and Aaron. "Now boys, attention. The cradle and Polly Woodley are nothing to you. We will proceed with what we were about."

"Please, sir," said Tom Metters, thrusting forth his hand as a semaphore, "what do Quinquagesima, Septuagesima and the lot of they rummy names mean?"

"Rummy," reproved Captain Tubb, "is an improper term to employ. Say, remarkable. Quinquagesima"—he stroked his moustache, then brightened—"it is the name of a Sunday."

"I know, sir, but why is it so called?"

"Why are *you* called Tom Metters?" asked the captain as a feeble effort to turn the tables.

"I be called Tom after my uncle, and Metters is my father's name—but Quinquagesima?"

"Quin-qua-gess-im-a!" mused the Captain,

and looked furtively towards my lady for help, but she was engrossed in teaching her class what books were not to be employed for the establishment of doctrine, and did not notice the appeal.

"Yes, sir," persisted Metters, holding him as a ferret holds the throat of a rabbit, "Quinquagesima."

"I think," said Tubb eagerly, "we were engaged on David's mighty men. Go on with the mighty men."

"But, please sir, I *do* want to know about Quinquagesima, cruel bad."

"Quin-qua-gess-ima," sighed Capt. Tubb, nibbling the ends of his beard; then again in a lower sigh, "Quin-qua-gess-ima?" He looked at Arminell for enlightenment, but in vain. She was listening amused and scornful.

"Gessima—gessima!" said Mr Tubb; then falteringly: "It's a sort of creeper, over veranders."

He saw a flash in Arminell's eye, and took it as encouragement. Then, with confidence he advanced.

'Yes, Metters, it means that this is the

Sunday or week whereabouts the yaller jessa-
mine—or in Latin, gessima—do begin to
bloom."

" Thank you, sir—and Septuagesima ? "

" That," answered the captain with great
promptitude, " that is when the white 'un
flowers."

" But, sir, there's another Sunday collick,
Sexagesima. There's no red or blue jessa-
mine, be there ? "

" Red, or blue ! " The teacher looked
hopelessly at Arminell, who with compressed
lips observed him and shook her head.

" Sex—sex—sex," repeated Mr. Tubb,
with his mouth full of beard, " always means
females. That means the female jessa-
mine."

" Be there any, sir ? There's a petticoat
narcissus, and a lady's smock, and a mary-
gold, but I never heard of a she-jessamine."

" There are none here," answered Tubb,
" but in the Holy Land—lots."

" Really, Arminell," said Lady Lamerton,
" your class is doing nothing but play and disturb mine."

"I am on the stool of the learner," sneered the girl.

At that moment, through the ceiling, or rather boards above, dropped a black-handled kitchen fork within a hair's breadth of Arminell's head. She drew back, startled.

"What is it? What is the matter?" exclaimed Lady Lamerton. "Run up, Polly Woodley!—no, not you this time; you, Fanny White, and see what they are about upstairs."

"Please, my lady," said Polly, peering into the higher regions through the hole, " Bessie have given the baby the knives and forks to play with, 'cause you wont let her rock the cradle, and to keep 'un from crying. He's a shoving 'em through the floor."

Then, down through the knot-hole descended a shower of comfits. The child had been given a cornet by its mother, and had eagerly opened it, over the hole where it had poked the fork.

The school floor was overspread with a pink and white hail-shower. In a moment, all order was over. The classes broke up into individual units, all on the floor, kicking, scratching, elbowing, grabbing after the scattered comfits, thrusting fingers into eyes, into soapy water; getting them trodden on, nipped between slates, a wriggling, contending, greedy, noisy tangle of small humanity, and above it stood my lady protesting, and Captain Tubb nibbling the ends of his sandy beard, and looking dazed; and Arminell Inglett, half angry, half amused, altogether contemptuous.

'There!" exclaimed Lady Lamerton, "the bells are going for divine service. In places at once—Let us pray!"

CHAPTER II.

THE church bells were ringing, the Sunday-school had at last been reduced to order, arranged in line, and wriggled, sinuous, worm-like, along the road and up the avenue to the church porch. Lady Lamerton, brandishing her sunshade as a field-marshal's baton, kept the children in place, and directed the head of the procession.

But with what heart-burnings, what envies, what excited passions did that train sweep on its way. Some of the children had got more comfits than others, and despised those less favoured by luck, and others comfitless envied the more successful. Polly Woodley had secured more comfits than the rest, and had them screwed in the corner of her pocket-handkerchief, and she thrust it exultantly under the eyes of Fanny White, who had come off with one only.

Some sobbed because they had crumpled their gowns, one boy howled because in stooping he had ruptured his nether garments, Joan Ball had broken the feather in her hat, and revenged herself on her neighbour by a stab of pin. One child strewed its tongue with comfits, and when Lady Lamerton did not observe, exposed its tongue to the rest of the children to excite their envy. Another was engaged in wiping out of its eyes the soapy water that in the scuffle had been squirted into them.

Captain Tubb dropped away at the church gates to shake hands with, and talk to, some of the villagers, the inn-keeper to the Lamerton Arms, the churchwarden, the guardian of the poor, and the miller, men who constituted the middle crumb of the parochial loaf.

Lady Lamerton likewise deserted her charges at the porch, and having consigned them to the clerk, returned on her course, entered the drive, and proceeded to meet his lordship, that they might make their solemn entrance into church together. Arminell had disappeared.

"Where is the girl?" asked her ladyship when she took my lord's arm.

"Haven't seen her, my dear."

"Really, Lamerton," said my lady, "she frightens me. She is so impulsive and self-willed. She flares up when opposed, and has no more taste for Sunday-school than I have for oysters. I do my best to influence her for good, but I might as well try to influence a cocoa-nut. By the way, Lamerton, you really must build us a Sunday-school, the inconveniences to which we are subjected are intolerable."

"Have you seen Legassick, my dear?"

"I believe he is standing by the steps."

"I must speak to him about the road, it has been stoned recently. Monstrous! It should have been metalled in he winter, then the stones would have worked in, now they will be loose all the summer to throw down the horses."

"And you will build us a Sunday-school?

"I will see about it. Wont the keeper's lodge do? The woman does not wash downstairs on a Sunday."

" I wish you kept school there one Sabbath day. You would discover how great are the discomforts. Now we are at the church gates and must compose our minds."

" Certainly, my dear. The lord-lieutenant is going to make Gammon sheriff."

" Why Gammon ? "

" Because he can afford to pay for the honour. The old squirearchy can't bear the expense."

" Hush, we are close to the church, and must withdraw our minds from the world."

" So I will, dear. Eggin's pigs have been in the garden again."

" There'll be the exhortation to-day, Lamerton, and you must stand up for it. Next Sunday is Sacrament Sunday."

" To be sure. I'll have a lower line of wire round the fences. Those pigs go where a hare will run."

" Have you brought your hymnal with you ? "

Lord Lamerton fumbled in his pocket, and produced his yellow silk kerchief and a book together.

" That," said his wife, " is no good ; it is
the old edition."

" It doesn't matter. I will open the book,
and no one will be the wiser."

" But you will be thinking during the hymn
of Eggin's pigs and Gammon's sheriffalty."

" I'll do better next Sunday. The
gardener tells me they have turned up your
single dahlias."

" Hush ! we are in the church. Arminell
is not in the pew. Where can she be ? "

Arminell was not in church. She was, in
fact, walking away from it, and by the time
her father had entered his pew and looked
into his hat, had put a distance of half a mile
between herself and the sacred building. A
sudden fit of disgust at the routine of Sunday
duties had come over her, and she resolved
to absent herself that morning from church,
and pay a visit to a deserted lime quarry, where
she could spend an hour alone, and her moral
and religious sense, as she put it, could recover tone after the ordeal of Sunday-school.

" What can induce my lady to take a class
every Sunday ? " questioned Arminell in her

thought. "It does no good to the children, and it maddens the teachers. But, oh! what a woman mamma is! Providence must have been hard up for ideas when it produced my lady. How tiresome!"

These last words were addressed to a bramble that had caught in her skirt. She shook her gown impatiently and walked on. The bramble still adhered and dragged.

"What a nuisance," said Arminell, and she whisked her skirt round and endeavoured to pick off the brier, but ineffectually.

"Let me assist you," said a voice; and in a moment a young man leaped the park wall, stepped on the end of the bramble, and said, "Now, if you please, walk on, Miss Inglett."

Arminell took a few steps and was free. She turned, and with a slight bow said, "I thank you, Mr. Saltren." Then, with a smile, "I wish I could get rid of all tribulations as easily."

"And find them whilst they cling as light. You are perhaps not aware that 'tribulation' derives from the Latin *tribulus*, a bramble."

"So well aware was I that I perpetrated

the joke which you have spoiled by threshing it. Why are you not at church, Mr. Saltren, listening for the rector's pronunciation of the Greek names of St. Paul's acquaintances, in the hopes of detecting a false quantity among them?"

"Because Giles has a cold, and I stay at my lady's desire to read the psalms and lessons to him."

"I wonder whether schooling Giles is as intolerable as taking Sunday class; if it be, you have my grateful sympathy."

"Your sympathy, Miss Inglett, will relieve me of many a tribulus which adheres to my robe."

"Is Giles a stupid boy and troublesome pupil?"

"Not at all. My troubles are not connected with my little pupil."

"Class-taking in that Sunday-school is a sort of mental garrotting," said Arminell. "I wonder whether a teacher always feels as if his brains were being measured for a hat when he is giving instruction."

"Only when there is non-receptivity in

the minds of those he teaches, or tries to
teach. May I ask if you are not going to
church, Miss Inglett?"

" I have done the civil by attending the
Sunday-school, and the articles disapprove of
works of supererogation. I am going to
worship under the fresh green leaves, and to
listen to the choir of the birds—blackbird,
thrush, and ouzel. I am too ruffled in temper
to sit still in church and listen to the same
common-places in the same see-saw voice
from the pulpit. Do you know what it is to
be restless, Mr. Saltren, and not know what
makes you ill at ease? To desire greatly
something, and not know what you long
after?"

The young man was walking beside her,
a little in the rear, respectfully, not full
abreast. He was a pale man with an oval
face, dark eyes and long dark lashes, and a
slight downy moustache.

" I can in no way conceive that anything
can be lacking to Miss Inglett," he said.
" She has everything to make life happy, an
ideally perfect lot, absolutely deficient in

every element that can jar with and disturb
tranquillity and happiness."

"You judge only by exterior circumstances.
You might say the same of the bird in the
egg — it fits it as a glove, it is walled
round by a shell against danger, it is warmed
by the breast of the parent, why should it be
impatient of its coiled up, comatose condition? Simply because that condition is
coiled up and comatose. Why should the
young sponge ever detach itself from the
rock on which it first developed by the side
of the great absorbent old sponge? It gets
enough to eat, it is securely attached by its
foot to the rock ; it is in the oceanic level
that suits its existence. Why should it let
go all at once and float away, rise to the
surface and cling elsewhere? Because of the
monotony of its life of absorption and contraction, and of its sedentary habits. But,
there,—enough about myself ; I did not in-
tend to speak of myself. You have brambles
clinging to you. Show me them, that I may
put my foot on them and free you."

"You know, Miss Inglett, who I am—the

son of the captain of the manganese mine, and that his wife is an old lady's maid from the park. You know that I was a clever boy, and that his lordship most generously interested himself in me, and when it was thought I was consumptive, sent me for a couple of winters to Mentone. You know that he provided for my schooling, and sent me to the University, and then most kindly took me into Orleigh as tutor to your half-brother Giles, till I can resolve to enter the Church, when, no doubt, he will some day give me a living. All that you know. Do not suppose I am insensible to his lordship's kindness, when I say that all this goodness shown me has sown my soul full of brambles, and made me the most miserable of men."

" But how so?" Miss Inglett looked at him with unfeigned surprise. " As you said to me, so say I to you, and excuse the freedom. Mr. Saltren has everything to make life happy, education, comfortable quarters, kind friends, an assured future, an ideally perfect lot, absolutely deficient in disturbing elements."

"Now you judge by the outside. I admit to the full that Lord Lamerton has done everything he could think of to do me good, but can one man calculate what will suit another? Will a bog plant thrive in loam, or a heath in clay?"

"You do not think that what has been done for you is well done?"

"I am not inclined for the Church, I have a positive distaste for the ministry, and yet Lord Lamerton is bent on my being a parson. If I do not become one, what am I to be? I cannot go back to the life whence I have been taken; I cannot endure to be with those who hold their knives by the middle when eating, and drink their tea out of their saucers, and take their meals in their shirt sleeves. Remember I have been translated from the society to which by birth I belong, to another as different from it as is that of Brahmins from Esquimaux; I cannot accommodate myself again to what was once my native element. Baron Munchausen, in one of his voyages, landed on an island made of cream cheese, and only discovered it by the fainting of a

sailor who had a natural antipathy to cream
cheese. I have come ashore on an island the
substance of which is altogether different from
the soil where I was born. I cannot say I
have an ineradicable distaste for it, but that
at first I found a difficulty in walking on it.
The specific gravity of cream cheese is other
than that of clay. Now that I have acquired
the light and trippant tread that suits, if I
return to my native land, my paces will be
criticised, and regarded as affected, and myself as supercilious, for not at once plodding
from my shoulders like a ploughboy in marl.
How was it with poor Persephone who spent
half her time in the realm of darkness and
half in that of light? She carried to the world
of light her groping tentative walk, and was
laughed at, and when in Hades, she trod
boldly as if in day and got bruises and bloody
noses. Even now I am in a state of oscillation
between the two spheres, and am at home in
neither, miserable in both. When I am in
the cream-cheese island I never feel that I can
walk with the buoyancy of one born on cream-
cheese. I can never quite overcome the sense

of inhaling an atmosphere of cheese, never quite find the buttermilk squeezed out of it taste like aniseed water."

Arminell could not refrain from a laugh. " Really, Mr. Saltren, you are not complimentary to our island."

"Call it the Isle of Rahat la Koum, Turkish Delight, or Guava Jelly—anything luscious. One who has eaten salt pork and supped vinegar cannot at once tutor his palate to everything saccharine to a syrup."

" But what really troubles you in the Isle of Guava ? "

" I am not a native but a stranger. Your tongue is by me acquired. There are even tones and inflexions of voice in you I cannot attain because my vocal organs got set in another world. A man like myself taken up and carried into a different sphere by another hand is inevitably so self-conscious that his self-consciousness is a perpetual torment to him. According to the apocryphal tale, an angel caught Habakkuk by the hair and carried him with a mess of pottage in his hands through the air, and deposited him in

Daniel's den of lions. Your father has been my angel, who has taken me up and transported me, and now I am in a den of lordly beasts who stalk round me and wonder how I came among them, and turn up their noses at the bowl I carry in my shaking hands."

"And you want to escape from us lions?"

"Pardon me—I am equally ill at ease elsewhere, I have associated with lions till I can only growl."

"And lash yourself raw," laughed Arminell; "you know a lion has a nail at the end of his tail, wherewith he goads himself."

"I can torture myself— that is true," said Saltren, in a disquieted tone. "My lord will give me a living and provide for me if I will enter the Church, but that is precisely an atmosphere I do not relish—and what am I to do? I cannot dig, to beg I am ashamed."

"Mr. Saltren, you are not at ease in the lions' den, but suppose you were to crawl out and get into the fields?"

"I should lose my way, having been carried

by the angel out of my own country. You
see the wretchedness of my position, I am
uncomfortable wherever I am. In my present
situation I imagine slights. Anecdotes told
at table make me wince, jokes fret me. Conversation on certain subjects halts because I
am present. Yet I cannot revert to my native
condition ; that would be deterioration, now I
have acquired polish, and have progressed."

" I should not have supposed, Mr. Saltren,
that you were so full of trouble."

"No—looking on a rose-pip, all smoothness,
you do not reckon on its being full of choke
within. And now—Miss Inglett, you see at
once an instance of my lack of tact and knowledge. I am in doubt whether I have done
well to pour out my pottle of troubles in your
ear, or whether I have behaved like a
booby."

" I invited you to it."

" Precisely, but in the language of the Isle
of Guava, words do not mean what they are
supposed to mean in the Land of Bacon. I
may have transgressed those invisible bounds
which you recognise by an instinct of which

I am deficient. There are societies which
have laws and signs of fellowship known only
to the initiated. You belong to one, the
great Freemasonry of Aristocratic Culture.
You all know one another in it, how—is inconceivable to me, though I watch and puzzle
to find the symbol ; and your laws, unwritten,
I can only guess at, but you all know them,
suck them in with mother's milk. I have
been brought up among you, but I have only
an idea of your laws, and as for your shibboleth
—it escapes me altogether. And now—I do
not know whether I have acted rightly or
wrongly in telling you how I am situated. I
am in terror lest in taking you at your word I
may not have grossly offended you, and lest
you be now saying in your heart, What an
unlicked cub this is ! how ignorant of tact, how
lacking in good breeding ! He should have
passed off my invitation with a joke about
brambles. He bores me, he is insufferable."

"I assure you—Mr. Saltren——"

"Excuse my interrupting you. It may,
or may not be so. I dare say I am hyper-
sensitive, over-suspicious."

"And now, Mr. Saltren, I think Giles is waiting for his psalms and lessons."

"You mean—I have offended you."

"Not at all. I am sorry for you, but I think you are—excuse the word—morbidly sensitive."

"You cannot understand me because you have never been in my land. Baron Munchausen says that in the moon the aristocrats when they want to know about the people send their heads among them, but their trunks and hearts remain at home. The heads go everywhere and return with a report of the wants, thoughts and doings of the common people. You are the same. You send your heads to visit us, to enquire about us, to peep at our ways, and search out our goings, but you do not understand us, because you have not been heart and body down to finger-ends and toes among us, and of us—you cannot enter into our necessities and prejudices and gropings. But I see, I bore you. In the tongue of the Isle of Guava you say to me, Giles wants his psalms and lessons. Which being interpreted means,

This man is a bramble sticking to my skirts, following, impeding my movements, a drag, a nuisance. I must get rid of him. I wish you a good morning, Miss Inglett ; and holy thoughts under the greenwood tree !"

CHAPTER III

IN THE OWL'S NEST.

Armorel Inglott made the best of her way to the old quarry. She was impatient to be abroad, to enjoy the beautiful weather, the spring sights and sounds to recover the elasticity of spirit of which she had been robbed by Sunday-school.

But would she recover that elasticity after her conversation with the young curate? What he had said was true. He was a village lad of humble antecedents who had been taken up by her father because he was intelligent and pleasing, and commended by the schoolmaster and delicate. Lord and Lady Lawrence were ever ready to do a kindness to a ...... or inhabitant of Oxleigh. When any of the latter were sick they received jellies and soups and the best port wine from the park; and a deserving child in school received recognition, and a steady youth was sure of a helping hand into a good situation.

More than ordinary favour had been shown to this young **man, son** of Stephen Saltren, captain of the manganese mine. He had been lifted out of the station in which he had been born, and was promoted to be the instructor of Giles. Arminell had always thought **her** father's conduct towards him extraordinarily kind, and now her eyes were open to see that it had been a cruel kindness, filling the young man's heart with a bitter**ness that** contended with his gratitude.

It would have been more judicious perhaps had **Lord** Lamerton sent young Jingles elsewhere.

Jingles, it must be explained, was not the tutor's Christian name. He had been baptised out of compliment to his lordship, Giles Inglett, and Giles Inglett Saltren was his complete name. But in the national school his double Christian name had been condensed, not without a flavour of spite, into Jingles, and at Orleigh he would never **be** known by any other.

The old lime-quarry lay a mile from the park. It was a picturesque spot, and would have been perfectly beautiful but for the heaps of rubbish thrown out of it which took years to decay, and which till decayed were unsightly. The process had, however, begun. Indeed, as the quarry had been worked for a century prior to its abandonment, a good deal of the " ramp," as such rubbish heaps are locally called, was covered with grass and pines.

Lord Lamerton had done his best to disguise the nakedness by plantations of Scotch, larch and spruce, which took readily to the loose soil, the creeping roots grasped the nodes of stone and crushed them as in a vice, then sucked out of them the nutriment desired ; the wild strawberry rioted over the banks, and the blackberry brambles dropped their trailers over the slopes, laden in autumn with luscious fruit, and later, when flowers are scarce with frost-touched leaves, carmine, primrose, amber and purple.

At the back of the quarry was an old wood, sloping to the south and breaking off sharply at the precipice where the lime rock had been cut away ; this was a wood of oaks with an undergrowth of bracken and male fern, and huge hollies. Here and there large venerable Scotch pines rose above the rounded surface of the oak tops, in some places singly, elsewhere in dark clumps.

The rock of the hill was slaty. The strata ran down and made a dip and came to the surface again, and in the lap lay the limestone. When the quarry-men had deserted the old workings, water came in and partly filled it, to the depth of forty feet, with crystalline bottle-green water. Lord Lamerton had put in trout, and the fish grew there to a great size, but were too wary to be caught. The side of the quarry to the south shelved rapidly into the water, and the fisherman standing on the slope with his rod was visible to the trout. They were too cautious to approach, and too well fed with the midges that hovered over the water to care to bite.

The north face of the quarry—that is the face that looked to the sun—was quite precipitous; it rose to the same height above the water that it descended beneath it. Over the edge hung bushes of may that wreathed the gray rocks in spring with snow as of the past winter, and in winter with scarlet berries, reminiscences of the fire of lost summer. Where the may-bushes did not monopolise the top, there the heath and heather hung their wiry branches and grew to brakes, and the whortleberry—the vaccinium— formed a fringe of glossy leafage in June and July rich with purple berries, and in autumn dotted with fantastic scarlet, where a capricious leaf had caught a touch of frost that had spared its fellows.

Down a rocky cranny fell a dribbling stream, the drainage of the wood above ; in summer it was but a distillation, sufficient to moisten the beds of moss and fern that rankly grew on the ledges beneath it, and in winter never attaining sufficient volume to dislodge the vegetation it nourished.

To the ledges thus moistened choice ferns had retreated as to cities of refuge from the rapacity of collectors, who rive away these delicate creatures regardless what damage is

done them, indifferent whether they kill in
the process, considering only the packing of
them off in hampers for sale or barter, and in
many places exterminating the rarest and
most graceful ferns ; but here, with a gulf of
deep water between themselves and their
pursuers, the parsley and maiden-hair ferns
throve and tossed their fronds in security and
insolence.

It was marvellous to see how plants luxuri-
ated in this old abandoned quarry, how they
seized on it, as squatters on no-man's land,
and multiplied and grew wanton and revelled
there ; how the hart's tongue grew there to
enormous size, and remained, unbrowned by
frost, throughout the winter ; how the crane's
bill bloomed to Christmas, and scented the
air around, and the strawberry fruited out of
season and reason.

By what fatality did the butterflies come
there in such numbers ? Was it that they
delighted in dancing over the placid mirror
admiring themselves therein ? After a few
gyrations they inevitably dipped their wings
and were lost ; perhaps they mistook their gay

reflections for inviting flowers, or perhaps like Narcissus, they fell in love with their own likenesses, and, stooping to kiss, were caught.

In summer butterflies were always to be found hovering over or floating on the surface, but they hovered or floated only for a while, presently a ring was formed in the glassy surface, a ring that widened and multiplied itself—the butterfly was gone, and a trout the better for it.

About six feet of soil, in some places more, in others less, appeared in sections above the quarry-edge, that is to say, above the rock. It was quite possible to trace the primitive surface of the pre-historic earth, much indented ; but these indentations had been filled in by accumulations of humus, so that the upper turf was almost of a level.

Where rock ended and soil began, the jackdaws had worked for themselves caves and galleries in which they lived a communal life, and multiplied prodigiously. A pair of hawks bred there as well, spared by express order of Lord Lamerton, but viewed with bitter animosity by the keepers ; also a colony of white owls, all on tolerable terms, keeping their distances, avoiding social intercourse, very much like the classes among mankind. These owls also would have perished, nailed to the stable doors or the keeper's wall, had not his lordship extended protection to them likewise. The kingfishers in the Ore were becoming fewer, the keepers waged war on them also, because they interfered with the fish. Lord Lamerton did not know this, or he would have held his protecting hand over their amethystine heads.

The cliff was ribbed horizontally, the harder bands of stratification standing forth as shelves on which lodged the crumbling of the more friable beds, and the leaves that sailed down from the autumn trees above. On these ledges a few bushes and a stunted Scotch pine grew. The latter grappled with the rock, holding to it with its red-brown roots like the legs of a gigantic spider.

At the west end, on a level with the topmost shelf of rock, just beneath where the earth buried the surface of rock, was a cave artificially constructed, at the time when the lime was worked, as a refuge for the miners when blasting.

Formerly a path had existed leading to this cave, but now the path was gone—scarce a trace survived. The owls, calculating on the inaccessibility of the grot to man, had taken possession of it, and bred there.

"I am glad I came here," said Arminell. "In this lovely, lonely spot one can worship God better than in a stuffy church, pervaded with the smell of yellow-soap, of clean linen, and the bergamot of oiled heads, and the peppermint the clerk sucks. Here one has the air full of the incense of the woods, the pines exuding resin in the sun, the oak-leaves exhaling their aroma, and the ferns, fragrant with a sea-like stimulating odour. I am weary of that hum-drum which constitutes to mamma the law and aim of life. We may be all—as Jingles says—steeped in syrup, but it is the syrup of hum-drum that crystallizes about us, after having extracted from us and dismissed all individual flavour, like the candied fruit in a box, where currants, greengage, apricot, pear—all taste alike. We are so saturated with the same syrup that we all lead the same saccharine existences, have the same sweet thoughts, utter the same sugary words, and have not an individualizing smack and aroma among us. Mamma is the very incarnation of routine. She talks to her guests on what she thinks will interest them, got up for the occasion out of magazines and reviews. These magazines save her and the like of her a world of trouble. The aristocrats of the moon, according to Jingles, sent their heads forth in pursuit of knowledge ; we have other peculiar heads sent to us stuffed with the forced meat of knowledge, and wrapped in the covers of magazines. So much for my mother. As for my father, he neither takes in nor gives vent to ideas. He presents prizes at schools, opens institutes, attends committees, sits on boards, presides at banquets ; occasionally votes, but never speaks in the House ; his whole circle of interests is made up of highways, asylums and county bridges. In olden times, witches drew circles and set about them skulls and daggers, toads, and braziers, and within these circles wrought necromancy. My father's circle is that of hum-drum, set round with county and parochial institutions, with the sanitary arrangements carefully considered, and without the magic circle he works—nothing."

She was standing at the west end of the quarry, looking along the edge of the pre-cipice, on her left.

"I wonder," she mused, "whether it would be feasible to reach the owls."

Filled with this new ambition, she thought no more of the shortcomings of her father and step-mother.

"It would be possible, by keeping a cool head," she said.

"I should like to see what an owl's nest is like, and in that cave I can pay my Sunday devotions."

The shelf was not broad enough to allow of any one walking on it unsupported, even with a cool head.

In places, indeed, it broadened, and there lay a cushion of grass, but immediately it narrowed to a mere indication. The distance was not great, from whence Arminell stood, to the cave, some twenty-five feet, and a slip would entail a fall into the water beneath.

As the girl stood considering the possibilities and the difficulties, she noticed that streamers of ivy hung over the edge from the surface of the soil. She could not reach these, however, from where she stood. Were she to lay hold of them, she might be able to sustain herself whilst stepping along the ledge, just as if she were supported by a pendent rope.

"I believe it is contrivable," she said, "I see where the ivy springs at the root of an elder tree. I can find or cut a crooked stick, and thus draw the strands to me. How angry and indignant mamma would be, were she to see what I am about."

She speedily discovered a suitable stick, and with its assistance drew the pendent branches towards her. Then, laying hold of them, she essayed an advance on the shelf. The ivy-ropes were tough, and tenacious in their rooting into the ground. She dragged at them, jerked them, and they did not yield. She grasped them in her left hand, and cautiously stepped forward.

At first she had a ledge of four inches in width to rest her feet on, but the rock, though narrow, was solid, and by leaning her weight well on the ivy, and advancing on the tips of her feet, she succeeded, not without a flutter of heart, in passing to a broad patch of turf, where she was comparatively safe, and where, still clinging to the ivy, she drew a long breath.

The water, looked down on from above, immediately beneath her was blue; only in the shadows, where it did not reflect the light, was it bottle-green.

There was not a ripple on it. She had not dislodged a stone. She turned her eyes up the bank. She had no fear of the ropes failing her; they would not be sawn through, because they swung over friable earth, not jagged rock.

"Allons, avançons," said Arminell, with a laugh. She was excited, pleased with herself—she had broken out of the circle of humdrum.

The ledge was wide, where she stood, and she held to the rope to keep her from giddiness, rather than to sustain her weight.

After a few further steps, she paused. The shelf failed altogether for three feet, but beyond the gap was a terrace matted with cistus and ablaze with flower. Arminell's first impulse was to abandon her enterprise as hazardous beyond reason, but her second was to dare the further danger, and make a spring to the firm ground.

" This is the difference between me and my lady," said Arminell. " She—and my lord likewise—will not risk a leap—moral, social, or religious."

Then with a rush of impetuosity and im-patience, she swung herself across the gap, and landed safely on the bed of cistus.

" Would Giles ever be permitted the un-conventional ? " asked Arminell. " What a petit-maître he will turn out."

The Hon. Giles Inglett, her half-brother, aged ten, was, as already said, the only son of Lord Lamerton and heir-apparent to the barony.

From the cistus patch she crept, still cling-ing to the ivy, along the ledge that now bore indications of the path once formed on it, and presently, with a sense of defiance of danger, allowed herself to look down into the still water.

"After all, if I did go down, it would not be very dreadful—it is a reversed heaven. I would spoil my gown, but what of that? I have my allowance, and can spoil as many gowns as I choose within my margin. I wonder—would a fall from my social terrace be as easy as one from this—and lead to such trifling and reparable consequences?"

Then she reached the platform of the cave, let go the ivy-streamers, and entered the grotto.

The entrance was just high enough for Arminell to pass in without stooping. The depth of the cave was not great, ten feet. The sun shone in, making the nook cheerful and warm. Again Arminell looked down at the pond.

"How different the water seems according to the position from which we look at it Seen from one point it blazes with reflected light, and laughs with brilliance; seen from another it is infinitely sombre, light-absorbing, not light-reflecting. It is so perhaps with the world, and poor Jingles contemplates it from an unhappy point."

She seated herself on the floor at the mouth of the cave, and leaned her back against the side, dangling one foot over the edge of the precipice.

" The best of churches, the most inspiring shrine for holy thoughts—O, how lucky, I have in my pocket Gaboriau's 'Gilded Clique !'"

She wore a pretty pink dress with dark crimson velvet trimmings, but the brightest point of colour about Arminell was the blood-coloured cover of the English version of the French romance of rascality and crime.

Arminell had lost her mother at an age at which she could not remember her. The girl had been badly brought up, by governesses unequal to the task of forming the mind and directing the conscience of a self-willed intelligent girl.

She had changed her governesses often, and not invariably for the better. One indulged and flattered her, and set her cap at Lord Lamerton. She had to be dismissed. Then came a methodical creature, eminently conscientious, so completely a piece of animated clockwork, so incapable of acting or even thinking out of a set routine, that she drove Arminell into sullen revolt. After her departure, a young lady from Girton arrived, who walked with long strides, wore a pince-nez, was primed with slang, and held her nose on high to keep her pince-nez in place. She was dismissed because she whistled, but not before her influence, the most mischievous of all, had left its abiding impress on the character of the pupil.

This governess laughed at conventionalities, such as are the safeguards of social life, and sneered at the pruderies of feminine modesty. Her tone was sarcastic and sceptical.

Then came a young lady of good manners, but of an infinitely feeble mind, who wore a large fringe to conceal a forehead as retreating as that of the Neanderthal man. Arminell found her a person of infinite promise and no achievement. She undertook to teach Greek, algebra, and comparative anatomy, but could not spell "rhododendron."

When Lord Lamerton had married again,

the new wife shrank from exercising authority over the wayward girl, and sought to draw her to her by kindness. But Arminell speedily gauged the abilities of her step-mother, and became not actively hostile, but indifferent to her. Lady Lamerton was not a person to provoke hostility.

Thus the girl had grown up with mind unformed, judgment undisciplined, feelings impetuous and under no constraint, and with very confused notions of right and wrong. She possessed by nature a strong will, and this had been toughened by resistance where it should have been yielded to, and non-resistance where it ought to have been firmly opposed.

She had taken a class that Sunday in the school, as well as on the preceding Sunday, only at Lady Lamerton's urgent request, because the school-mistress was absent on a holiday.

And now Arminell, who had come to the Owl's Nest to pay her devotions to heaven, performed them by reading Gaboriau's " Gilded Clique."

CHAPTER IV.

A PRAYER-RAFT.

How long Arminell had been resting in her sunny nook above the water, reading the record of luxury, misery and vice, she did not know, for she became engrossed in the repulsive yet interesting tale, and the time slipped away, unperceived.

She was roused from her reading by the thought that suddenly occurred to her, quite unconnected with the story, that she had let go the strands of ivy when she reached the cave,—and in a moment her interest in the "Gilded Clique" ceased and she became alarmed about her own situation. In her delight at attaining the object of her ambition, she had cast aside the streamers without a thought that she might need them again, and they had reverted to their original position, beyond her reach. She could not venture along the strip of turf without their support, and she had not the crook with her, wherewith to rake them back within reach of her hand.

What was to be done? The charm of the situation was gone. Its novelty had ceased to please. Her elation at her audacity in venturing on the "path perilous" had sub- sided. To escape unassisted was impossible, and to call for assistance useless in a place so rarely visited.

"It does not much matter," said Arminell ; " I shall not have to spend a night among the owls. My lady when she misses me will send out a search-party, and Jingles will direct them whither to go for me. I will return to my book."

But Arminell could not recover her interest in the story of the " Gilded Clique." She was annoyed at her lack of prudence, for it had not only subjected her to imprisonment, but had placed her in a position somewhat ri- diculous. She threw down the book im- patiently and bit her lips.

" This is a lesson to me," she said, " not to make rash excursions into unknown regions without retaining a clue which will enable me to retrace my steps to the known. Cæsar may have been a hero when he burnt his ships, but his heroism was next akin to folly."

She sat with her hands in her lap, with a clouded face, musing on the chance of her speedy release. Then she laughed, "Like Jingles, I am in a wrong position, but unlike him, I am here by my own foolhardiness. He was carried by my lord into the eagle's nest. Like Sinbad, out of the valley of diamonds. But in the valley of diamonds there were likewise serpents. My lord swooped down on poor Jingles, caught him up, and deposited him in his nest on the heights for the young eagles to pull to pieces."

As she was amusing herself with this fancy, she observed a man by the waterside at the east or further end of the quarry, engaged in launching a primitive raft which he drew out of a bed of alder. The raft consisted of a couple of hurdles lashed together, on which an old pig-sty or stable door was laid. Upon this platform the man stationed himself when the raft was adrift, and with a

long oar sculled himself into the middle of
the pond.

What was his object? Had he seen
Arminell and was he coming to her assistance, concluding that she could be rescued
in no other fashion? On further observation
Arminell convinced herself that he had not
seen her and knew nothing of her predica-
ment and distress.

What was he about to do? To fish?

No—not to fish.

When the raft floated in the middle of the
tarn, the man laid down his oar, knelt on the
board and began to pray.

" Why——!" exclaimed the girl ; " that is
Captain Saltren, Jingles' father."

Captain Stephen Saltren, master of the
manganese mine, was a tall man, rather gaunt
and thin, and loosely compacted at the joints,
with dark hair, high cheek-bones and large,
deeply-sunken eyes. His features were
irregular and ill cut—yet it was impossible to
look at his face without being impressed with
the thought that he was no ordinary man.
His hands, though roughened and enlarged

by work, had long fingers, the indication of a
nervous temperament. He had, moreover,
one of those flexible voices which go far towards making a man an orator. He was
unaware of the value of his organ, he was
devoid of skill in using it ; but it was an im-
pressive voice when used in times of deep
emotion, thrilling those who heard it and
sweeping them into sympathy with the
speaker. His eyes were those of a mystic,
looking into a far-off sphere, esteeming the
world of sense as a veil, a painted film, disturbing, impeding distinct vision of the sole
realities that existed in the world beyond.

There was velvety softness in his dark
eyes, and gentleness in his flexible mouth,
and yet the least observant person speaking
with him could see that fire was ready to leap
out of those soft eyes on provocation, and that
the mouth could set with rigid determination
when his prejudices were touched.

The forehead of the man was of unusual
height. He had become partly bald, had
shed some of the hair above the brow, and
this had given loftiness to his forehead. Ther

were hollows between his temples and eye-
brows; his head was lumpy and narrow. Altogether it was an ill-balanced, but an interesting head.

The mystic, who at one time was a prominent feature in religious life, has almost
disappeared from among us, gone utterly out
of the cultured classes, gone from among the
practical mercantile classes, going little by
little from the lower beds of life, not expelled by
education but by the materialism that pene-
trates every realm of human existence. In time
the mystic will have become as extinct as the
dodo, the great auk, and the Caleb Balder-
stones. But there are mystics still—especially where there is a strain of Celtic blood, and
of this class of beings was Stephen Saltren.

The captain was in trouble, and whenever
he was in trouble or unhappy he had recourse
to prayer, and he prayed with most disengage-
ment on his raft. He came to the quarry
when his mind was disturbed and his heart
agitated, thrust himself out from land, and
prayed where he believed himself to be unobserved and unlikely to be interrupted.

The cause of his unrest on this occasion was the threat Lord Lamerton had uttered of closing the manganese mine. This mine had its adit, crushing mill and washing floors at but a short distance from the great house. About fifteen years previous, a mine had been worked on the estate that yielded so richly, that with the profits, Lord Lamerton had been able to clear off some mortgages. That lode was worked out. It had been altogether an extraordinary one, bunching, as it is termed, into a great mass of solid manganese, but this bunch, when worked out, ended without a trace of continuance. Then, as Lord Lamerton was assured, another came to the surface in the hill behind the mansion, and as he was in want of money, he reluctantly permitted the mine to be opened within a rifle shot of his house. The workings were out of sight, hidden by a plantation, and manganese mines make no great heaps of unsightly deposit; nevertheless, the mine was inconveniently near the place. It did not yield as it had promised, or as the experts had pretended it promised, and Lord Lamerton had lost all hope of making money by it. The vein was followed, but it never " bunched." Foreign competition affected the market, English manganese was under-sold, and Wheal Perseverance, as the mine was called, did not pay for the " working." Lord Lamerton annually lost money on it. Then he was informed that the lode ran under Orleigh gardens, and promised freely to " bunch " under the mansion . That is to say, he was asked to allow his house to be undermined. This decided his lordship, and he announced that the mine must be abandoned. Bunch or no bunch, he was not going to have his old place tunnelled under and brought about his ears, on the chance—the chimerical chance—of a few thousand pounds' worth of metal being extracted from the rock on which it stood.

To Lord Lamerton his determination seemed right and reasonable. The land was his. The royalties were his ; the house was his. Every man may do what he will with his own. If he has a penny in his pocket, he is at liberty to spend or to hoard it as he deems best.

But this decision of his lordship threatened ruin or something like ruin to a good many men who had lived on the mine, to families whereof the father worked underground, and the children above washing ore on the floors. The cessation of the mining would throw all these out of employ. It was known to the miners that manganese mines were everywhere unprofitable and were being abandoned. Where then should they look for employment?

It was open to bachelors to migrate to America, but what were the married men to do? The captain would feel the stoppage of the mine most of all. He had kept the accounts of the output, had paid the wages, and sold the metal. The miners might, indeed, take temporary work on the new line in course of construction, but that meant a change of life from one that was regular, whilst living in settled homes, to a wandering existence, to makeshift housing, separation from their families, and to association with demoralising and lawless companions. The captain, however, had not this chance within reach. He could not migrate, because he possessed the little house in which he lived, together with an acre of garden ground beside it, which his father had enclosed and reclaimed. Moreover, he was not likely to find work which gave him a situation of authority and superiority. Instead of being a master he must be content—if he found employ—to work as a servant. Hitherto, he had engaged and dismissed the hands, now he must become a hand—and be glad to be one—liable to dismissal.

It was natural that the men, and especially Saltren, should feel keenly and resent the closing of the mine. People see things as they affect themselves, and appreciate them only as they relate to their own affairs. I knew a man named Balhatchet who patented a quack medicine which he called his Heal-all, and this man never could be brought to see that the Fall of Man was a disaster to humanity, for, he argued, if there had been no fall, then no sickness, and therefore no place for Balhatchet's Heal-all.

According to " The Spectator," when the

news reached London that the King of
France was dead, "Now we shall have fish
cheaper," was the greeting the tidings evoked.
The miners were angry with the bleachers,
because they used German manganese instead of that raised in England, and angry
with the shippers for bringing it across the
sea. But above all, at this time, they were
inclined to resent the action of Lord
Lamerton in closing the mine, for by so
doing he was, as they put it, snatching the
bread out of their hungry mouths, whilst
himself eating cake. They did not believe
that undermining the great house would disturb its foundations. That was a mere
excuse. How could his lordship be sure that
undermining would crack his walls till he had
tried it ? And—supposing they did settle,
what of that ? They might be rebuilt. The
men had been told that his lordship had
painted the north wall with impenetrable,
anti-damp preparation, because on that side
of the house the paper in the rooms became
mildewed. If there was damp, what better
means of drying the house than undermining

it? Why should his lordship send many
pounds to London for damp-excluding paint,
when by spending the money in Orleigh he
might so drain the soil through a level under
the foundations that no moisture could
possibly rise?

Lord Lamerton had made a great deal of
money out of the first mine. He had provided good cottages for his tenants, the workmen, but so much worse if they were to be
turned out of them.

The mine had been christened Wheal
Perseverance, and what does perseverance
mean, but going on with what is begun? If
his lordship had not intended to carry on the
mine indefinitely, he should not have called it
Wheal Perseverance. When he gave it that
name he as much as promised to keep it
going always, and to stop it now was a breach
of faith. Was it endurable that Lord
Lamerton should close the mine? Who had
put the manganese in the rock? Was it Lord
Lamerton? What had the metal been run
there for but for the good of mankind, that it
might be extracted and utilized? God had car-

ried the lode under Orleigh Park before a
Lamerton was thought of. Was it justifiable
that one man through his aristocratic selfishness should interfere with the public good,
should contravene the arrangements of the
Creator? In the gospel the man who hid his
talent was held up to condemnation, but here
was a nobleman who sat down upon the
talent belonging to a score of hard-working
and necessitous men, desirous of extracting
it, and refused to permit them to do what God
had commanded. Was there not a fable about
a dog in the manger? Was not his lordship
a very dog in a manger, neither using the
manganese himself, nor allowing those who
desired to dig it out to put a pick into the
ground and disturb it? Maybe there was
a "bunch" under the state drawing-room
large enough to support a score of families
for three years, the men in meat and broad-
cloth, the women in velvets and jockey-club
essence. Lord Lamerton and Lady Lamerton begrudged them these necessaries of life.
The laws of the land, no doubt, were on the
side of the nobleman, but the law of God on

that of the labourer. The laws were imposed on the people by a House of Lords and the Queen, and therefore they would agitate for the abolition of an hereditary aristocracy and keep their hats on when next the National Anthem was played.

There were more mixed up in the matter than his lordship. Lord Lamerton did nothing without consulting the agent, Mr. Macduff. The abandonment of the mine was Macduff's doing. The reason was known to every one—Macduff was under the control of his wife. Mrs. Macduff was offended because the school children did not curtsey and touch their caps when she drove through the village in her victoria.

The rector also had a finger in this particular pie. He bore a spite against Captain Saltren, because the captain was not a churchman. Not a word had been said about stopping the lime-quarry. Oh no! of course not, for Captain Tubb taught in the Sunday-school. If Stephen Saltren had taken a class, nothing would have been said about discontinuing the mine. Therefore the miners resolved to join the Liberation Society and make an outcry for the disestablishment of the Church.

So the men argued—we will not say reasoned, and that is no caricature of their arguments, not reasonings, in similar cases. The uneducated man is always a suspicious man. He never believes in the reasons alleged, these are disguises to hide the true springs of action.

When his lordship was told how incensed the miners were, he made light of the matter. Pshaw! fiddlesticks! He was not going to have his dear old Elizabethan home in which he was born, and which had belonged to the Ingletts before they were peers, tumbled about his ears like a pack of cards, just because there was a chance of finding three ha'porth of manganese under it. The mine had been a nuisance for some years. The standing up to their knees in water had been injurious to the health of the girls, many of whom had died of decline. Wheal Perseverance was a bad school of morals, lads and lasses worked together there, and necessarily in a semi-nude condition. The schoolmaster and the Government Inspector had complained that the attendance at school was bad and irregular, for the children could earn money on the washing floors, and did not see the fun of sitting at desks earning nothing.

The miners had been a constant source of annoyance, they were all of them poachers, and had occasional fights with the keepers. The presence of the miners entailed the retention of extra keepers to protect the game, so that in this way also the mine proved expensive. Besides, the manganese dirtied the stream that flowed through the grounds, made it of a hideous tawny red colour, and spoiled the fishing not only in it, but in the river Ore, into which it discharged its turbid waters.

The miners were all radicals and dissenters, and he would be glad to be rid of them.

So every question has its two sides, equally plausible.

Stephen Saltren had been from boyhood shy, silent and self-contained. His only

book of study was the Bible, and his imagination was fired by its poetry and its
apocalyptic visions. His thoughts were cast
in Scriptural forms ; his early companions
had nick-named him the Methodist Parson.
But Saltren had never permanently attached himself to any denomination. The
Church was too ceremonious, he turned from
her in dislike. He rambled from sect to
sect seeking a dwelling-place, and finding
only a temporary lodging. For a while he
was all enthusiasm, and flowed with grace,
then the source of unction ran dry, and he
attributed the failure to deficiencies in the
community he had joined, left it to re-
commence the same round of experiences
and encounter the same disappointments in
another. As a young man he had worked
with his father at the original mine, Wheal
Eldorado, and on his father's death, had
continued to live in the house his father had
built on land he had appropriated. He continued to work at Eldorado, became captain
in his father's room, and when Eldorado
was exhausted, directed the works of Wheal

Perseverance. Every one spoke highly of
Stephen Saltren, as a steady, conscientious
man, truthful and of unimpeachable honesty.
But no one quite understood Saltren, he
made no friends, he sought none ; and he
left on all with whom he came in contact,
the impression that he was a man of very
abnormal character.

Whilst Adam slept, the help-mate was
formed and set by him. When he opened
his eyes, it was with a start and with something like terror that he saw Eve at his side.
He could not but believe he was still a prey
to dreams. Ever since that first meeting
love has come as a surprise on the sons of
Adam, has come on them when least prepared to resist its advance, and has never
been regarded in the first moment as a grave
reality.

Thousands of years have rolled their
course, and love has remained unchanged,
like the rose and the nightingale, neither
developing forward to some higher form of
activity, nor degenerating to one less gener
ous.

The diseases pass through endless modifications, varying in phenomena with every generation, changing their symptoms, disguising their nature, but the fever of love is always one and runs the identical course. Enthusiasts have sought to stifle it in hair-cloth, and reduce its virulence by vaccination with foreign matter, but it resists every effort to subdue it. Society has attempted to discipline it and turn it to practical ends. But love is a fire which will consume all bonds and snap them, and is only finally extinguished with a handful of clay, when the breast in which it has burnt is reduced, ashes to ashes, and dust to dust.

Unexpectedly, unaccountably, the fever laid hold of Stephen Saltren. He lost his heart to Marianne Welsh, who had been servant at the park, a handsome girl, with refinement of manner beyond her class.

He courted her for a month. She had left the great house for some unexplained reason, some folks said she was a liar, and had been dismissed because found out to be unreliable; others said she left because she was so good-looking that the rest of the maids were jealous of her and worried her out of her situation.

Whilst courting Marianne, Saltren was a charmed man. His vision of the spiritual world became clouded, and he was not sensible of the loss. A new world of unutterable delight, and of ideal beauty, clothed in rainbow colours and bathed in brilliant light, had unfurled before him and now occupied his perspective.

The acquaintanceship led at once to marriage. There was no delay. There was no occasion for delay. Saltren possessed his own house and land, and was in receipt of a good salary. The marriage ensued; and then another change came over Saltren. The new world of love and beauty, so real, faded as the mirage of the desert, disclosing desert and dead bones.

Seven months after the marriage, Marianne became the mother of a boy, and only Stephen knew that the son was not his own. A cruel act of treachery had been committed. Marianne had taken his name, not because

she loved him, but to hide her own dishonour.

When he knew how he had been deceived,
a barb entered Stephen's heart, and he was
never after free from its rankle. A fire was
kindled in his veins that smouldered and
gnawed its way outwards, certain eventually
to flare forth in some sudden and unexpected
outbreak. He became more reserved, more
dreamy, more fantastic than before his marriage, and more of an enigma to those with
whom he associated.

" Let the babe be christened Giles Inglett,"
said Marianne, "that has a distinguished
sound, none of your vulgar Jacks, and
Harrys, and Bills—besides, it will be taken
as a compliment at the park, and may be of
benefit to the little fellow afterwards."

Saltren shrugged his shoulders.

" It is your child, call it what you will."

The boy was brought up by Stephen as
his son, none doubted the paternity. But
Saltren never kissed the infant, never showed
the child love, took no interest in the welfare
of the youth. To his wife he was cold, stern

and formal. He allowed her to see that he
could never forgive the wrong that had been
done him.

So much for the past of Captain Stephen
Saltren. Now, on this spring Sunday morning, Arminell Inglett watched the man at his
devotions on the raft. She allowed him to
proceed with them undisturbed for some
time ; but she could not spend the whole day
in the owl's nest. Saltren must be roused
from his spiritual exercises and raptures.
He must assist her—he must surely have
ropes at his disposal, and could call men to
help in her release.

She called him by name.

Her call was re-echoed from the rocky
walls of the quarry. Saltren looked up,
looked about, and remained expectant, with
uplifted hands and eyes.

Then, half impatiently, half angrily,
Arminell flung the crimson-covered novel of
Gaboriau far out into the air, to fall on or
near Saltren, in the hopes of directing his
attention to her position.

He saw the fluttering book in the air, and

stretched forth his hands to receive it. The
book whirled about, expanded, turned over,
shut, and shot down into the pond, where it
floated one moment with its red cover upwards. Captain Saltren was engrossed
in interest to see and to secure the book, he
sculled towards it, stooped over the water
to grasp it, lost balance, and fell forward,
and in his effort to recover the volume
and save himself from immersion, touched
it, and the book went under the raft and
disappeared.

The attempt to attract attention to herself
had failed, and Arminell uttered an exclamation of vexation.

CHAPTER V.

INFECTION.

A TOUCH on Arminell's shoulder made her turn with a start. She saw behind her an old woman who had approached along the ledge, unobserved, supporting herself by the strands of ivy in the same manner as herself. Arminell had been standing leaning against the rock, her eyes and attention occupied with Captain Saltren, and so had not noticed the stealthy progress of the woman.

" See here, miss," said the new arrival, " I have come to help you in the proper way. Lord love y' what's the good o' calling to that half mazed man there? By the road you came, by that you must return. Here be ivy bands enough for both. Take half yourself and follow me, or if you'd rather, go on before. Don't look at your feet, look ahead."

" Who are you ? " asked Arminell in surprise.

" Won't you accept help till you know who she is that offers it ?" asked the woman with a laugh. " Do you object to lean on a stick till you know the name of the tree whence it was cut ? I'm not ashamed of what I'm called, I'm Patience Kite, that lives in the thatched cottage under the wood at the end of the quarry. I saw how you came to this place, and how you have thrown your book at the captain, because he looked every way but the right one when he was called. There's perversity in all things, miss, as you'll dis· cover when you're a bit older. Them as we call to come to us don't look our way, and them as we ain't thinking about offer us the helping hand."

Arminell took the proffered ivy ropes, and began to retrace her steps along the face of the precipice, but was unable, whilst so doing, to resist the temptation to look and see if Captain Saltren had as yet observed her, but she saw that he was still diving his arms into the water after the sunken volume, and was unconscious that any one watched him.

" Hold to my gown, it is coarse, but the

better to stay you with," said the woman. " Do not look round, keep fast with the right hand to the ivy, and clutch me with your left. What a comical bringing together of them whom God has put asunder that would be if you and I were to be found in death grappled together in the quarry pond ! "

Slowly, cautiously, Arminell followed her guide and finally reached the firm bank.

" Now then," said Patience, " you can come and rest in my cottage. It is hard by. I'll wipe a chair for you. As you wanted to see the owl's nest, perhaps you mayn't object to visit the house of the white witch."

Arminell hesitated. She was inclined to return home, but felt that it would seem ungracious to decline the offer of the woman who had assisted her out of her difficulties.

" Look yonder," mocked Patience, pointing to the water, " the captain is at his prayers again. I wonder, now, what he took that book to be you throwed at him, and your voice to be that called him ? He'll make a maze o' queer fancies out of all, I reckon."

" Does Mr. Saltren often come here ? "

F

"When the shoe pinches."

"I do not understand you, Mrs. Kite."

"No, I'll be bound you do not. How can you understand the pinching and pain o' others, when you've never felt pinch or pain yourself? Such as lie a-bed in swans' down wonder what keeps them awake that couches on nettles."

"But what has this to do with Captain Saltren and his prayers?"

"Everything," answered the woman; "you don't ask for apples when your lap is full. Those that suffer and are in need open their mouths. But whether aught comes to them for opening their mouths is another matter. The cuckoo in my clock called, and as none answered, he gave it up—so did I."

There was a savagery in the woman's tone that startled Arminell, and withal a strangeness in her manner that attracted her curiosity.

"I will go with you to the cottage for a moment," she said.

"This is the way," answered Patience, leading through the brake of fern under the oaks.

Patience Kite was a tall woman, with black hair just turning grey, a wrinkled face, and a pointed chin. She had lost most of her teeth, and mouthed her words, but spoke distinctly. Her nose was like the beak of a hawk; her eyes were grey, and wild under heavy dark brows. When she spoke to Arminell she curtsied, and the curtsey of the gaunt creature was grotesque. The girl could not read whether it were intended as respectful, or done in mockery. Her dress was tidy, but of the poorest materials, much patched. She wore no cap; her abundant hair was heaped on her head, but was less tidy than her clothing; it was scattered about her face and shoulders.

Her cottage was close at hand, very small, built of quarry-stone that corroded rapidly with exposure—the air reduced it to black dust. The chimney threatened to fall; it was gnawed into on the south-west side like a bit of mice-eaten cheese. The thatch was rotten, the rafters were exposed and decayed. The walls, bulged out by the thrust of the bedroom floor-joists,

were full of rents and out of the perpendicular.

The place looked so ruinous, so unsafe,
that Arminell hesitated to enter.

The door had fallen, because the frame
had rotted away.   Patience led her guest
over it into the room.   There everything was
tidy and clean.   Tidiness and cleanliness
were strangely combined with ruin and decay.
In the window was a raven in a cage.

"This house is dangerous to live in," said
Arminell.   "Does Mr. Macduff not see that
repairs are done?   It is unfit for human
habitation."

"Macduff!" scoffed Mrs. Kite.   "Do
y' think that this house belongs to his lordship?   It is mine, and because it is mine
they cannot force me to leave it, and to go
into the workhouse."

"But you are in peril of your life here,
the chimney might fall and bury you any
windy night.   The roof might crash in."

"So the sanitary officer says.   He has
condemned the house."

"Then you are leaving?"

" No. He has done his duty. But I am not going to turn out."

" Yet surely, Mrs. Kite, if the place is dangerous, you will not be allowed to remain ? "

" Who can interfere with me ? The board of guardians have applied to the petty sessions for an order, and it has been granted and served on me."

" Then, of course, you go ? "

" No ; they can order me to go, but they cannot force me to go. The policeman says they can fine me ten shillings a day if I remain and defy them. Let them fine me. They must next get an order to distrain to get the amount. They may sell my furniture, but they won't be able to turn me out."

" But why remain in peril of your life ? You will be crushed under the ruins some stormy night."

" Why remain here ? Because I've nowhere else to go to. I will not go into the union, and I will not live in a house with other folk. I am accustomed to be alone. I am not afraid. Here I am at liberty, and I will die here rather than lose my freedom."

" You cannot even shut your door."

" I do not need to. I fear nothing, not the sanitary officer ; he can do nothing. Not the board of guardians ; they can do nothing. Not the magistrates ; they cannot touch me."[1]

" Have you anything to live on ? "

" I pick up a trifle. I bless bad knees and stop the flow of blood, and show where stolen goods are hidden, and tell who has ill-wished any one."

" You receive contributions from the superstitious."

" I get my living my own way. There is room for all in the world."

Arminell seated herself in a chair offered

---

[1] The reader may think this an impossible case. At the present moment an old woman in the author's immediate neighbourhood is thus defying all the authorities. They have come to a dead lock. She has resisted orders to leave for three years, and is in hourly peril of her life. The only person who could expel her is the landlord, who happens to be poor, and who says that he cannot rebuild the cottage, the woman who has it on a lease is bound to deliver it over at the end of the time in good order, but she is without the means to put the cottage in order. Next equinoctial gale may see her crushed to death.

her, and looked at the raven in its cage, picking at the bars.

Silence ensued for a few minutes. Patience folded her bare brown arms across her bosom, and standing opposite the girl, studied her from head to foot.

" The Honourable Miss Inglett ! " she said, and laughed. " Why are you the honourable, and I the common person ? Why are you a lady, at ease, well-dressed, and I a poor old creature badgered by sanitary officers and board of guardians, and magistrates, and by my lord, the chairman at the petty sessions ? "

Arminell looked wonderingly at her, surprised at her strange address.

" Because the world is governed by injustice. What had you done as a babe, that you should have the gold spoon put into your mouth, and why had I the pewter one ? It is not only sanitary officers and guardians of the poor against me, bullying me, a poor lone widow. Heaven above has been dead set against me from the moment I was born. I've seen the miners truck out ore and cable ; now a truck load of metal, then one of refuse ; one to be refined, the other to be rejected. It is so in life ; we are run out of the dark mines of nothingness into light, and some of us are all preciousness and some all dross. But do you know this, Miss Arminell, they turned out heaps on heaps of refuse from the copper mines, and now they have abandoned the copper to work the refuse heaps. They find them rich—in what do you suppose ? In arsenic."

"You have had much trouble in your life ?" asked Arminell, not knowing what to say to this strange, bitter woman.

" Much trouble !" Patience curtsied. She unlaced her arms, and used her hands as she spoke, like a Frenchwoman. She lacked the words that would express her thoughts, and enforced and supplemented them with gesture. " Much trouble ! You shall hear how I have been served. My father worked in this old lime quarry till it was abandoned, and when it stopped, then he was out of work for two months, and he went out poaching, and shot himself instead of a pheasant. He was not used to a gun. 'Twasn't the fault of the gun. The gun was good enough. When he was brought home dead, my mother went into one fainting fit after another, and I was born ; but she died."

" The quarry was given up, I suppose, because it was worked out ? " said Arminell.

" Why did Providence allow it to be worked out so soon ? Why wasn't the lime made to run ten feet deeper, three feet, one foot would have done it to keep my father alive over my birth, and so saved my mother's life and made me a happy woman ? "

" And when your poor mother died ? "

" Then it was bad for poor me. I was left an orphan child and was brought up by my uncle, who was a local preacher. He wasn't over-pleased at being saddled wi' me to keep. He served me bad, and didn't give me enough to eat. Once he gave me a cruel beating because I wouldn't say ' Forgive us our trespasses,' for, said I, ' Heaven has trespassed against me, not I against Heaven.' Why was there not another foot or eighteen inches more lime created when it

was made, so that my father and mother
might have lived, and I had a home and not
been given over to uncle? What I said then,
I say now "—all Patience's fierceness rushed
into her eyes. "Answer me. Have I been
fairly used?" She extended her arms, and
held her hands open, appealing to Arminell
for her judgment.

"And then?" asked the girl, after a long
silence, during which nothing was heard but
the pecking of the raven at the bars.

"And then my uncle bade me unsay my
words, but I would not. Then he swore he
would thrash me every day till I asked for-
giveness. So it came about."

"What came about?"

"That I was sent to prison."

"Not for profanity! for what?"

"For setting fire to his house."

"You—— ?"

"Yes, finish the question. Yes, I did;
and so I was sent to prison."

Arminell involuntarily shrank from the
woman.

"Ah! I frighten you. But the blame

does not attach to me. Why were there not a few inches more lime created when the quarry was ordained? Providence means, I am told, fore-seeing. When the world was made I reckon it was foreseen that for lack of a little more lime my father would shoot himself, and the shock kill my mother, and cast me without parents on the hands of a hard uncle, who treated me so bad that I was forced to set his thatch in a blaze, and so was sent to prison. Providence saw all that in the far-off, and held hands and did not lay another handful of lime."

"Have you ever been married?" asked Arminell, startled by the defiance, the rage and revolt in the woman's heart. She asked the question without consideration, in the hope of diverting the thoughts of Mrs. Kite into another channel.

Patience was silent for a moment, and looked loweringly at the young lady, then answered abruptly, "No—a few inches of lime short stopped that."

"How did that prevent your marriage? The quarry was stopped before you were born."

" Right, and because stopped, my father was shot and I became an orphan, and was took by my uncle, and fired his house, and was sent to gaol. After that no man cared to take to wife a woman who put lighted sticks among the thatch. No respectable man would share his name with one who had been in prison. But I was a handsome girl in my day—and—but there—I will tell you no more. The stopping of the quarry did it. If there had been laid at the bottom a few inches more of lime rock, it would never have happened. Where lies the blame?"

" Another quarry was opened," said Arminell, " that where Mr. Tubb is captain."

" True," answered Patience ; " but between the closing of one and the opening of another, my father bought a gun, and went over a hedge with it on a moonlight night, and the trigger caught."

Arminell rose.

" I have been here for some time," she said, " and I ought to be on my way home. You will permit me—" she felt in her pocket for her purse.

" No," said Patience curtly. " You have
paid me for what I did by listening to my
story. But stay—Have you heard that if
you go to a pixy mound, and take the soil
thereof and put it on your head, you can see
the little people, and hear their voices, and
know all they say and do. You have come
here—to this heap of ruin and wretchedness,"
she stooped and gathered up some of the
dust off the floor and ashes from the hearth,
and threw them on the head of Arminell. " I
am a witch, they say. It is well ; now your
eyes and ears are opened to see and know
and feel with those you never knew of before
this day—another kind of creatures to yourself—the poor, the wretched, the lonely."

CHAPTER VI.

CHILLACOT.

ARMINELL INGLETT walked musingly from the cottage of Patience Kite. The vehemence of the woman, the sad picture she had unfolded of a blighted life, the look she had been given into a heart in revolt against the Divine government of the world, united to impress and disturb Arminell.

Questions presented themselves to her which she had never considered before. Why were the ways of Heaven unequal? Why, if God created all men of one flesh, and breathed into all a common spirit, why were they differently equipped for life's journey? Why were some sent to encounter the freezing blast in utter nakedness, and others muffled in eider-down? The Norns who spin the threads of men's lives, spin some of silk and others of tow. The Parcæ who shovel the lots of men out of bushels of gold, dust and soot, give to some soot only; they do not trouble themselves to mix the ingredients before allotting them.

As Arminell walked on, revolving in her mind the perplexing question which has ever remained unsolved and continues to puzzle and drive to despair those in all ages who consider it, she came before the house of Captain Saltren.

The house lay in a narrow glen, so narrow that it was lighted and warmed by very little sun. A slaty rock rose above it, and almost projected over it. This rock, called the Cleve, was crowned with heather, and ivy scrambled up it from below. A brook brawled down the glen below the house.

The coombe had been wild and disregarded, a jungle of furze and bramble, till Saltren's father settled in it, and no man objecting, enclosed part of the waste, built a house, and called it his own. Lord Lamerton owned the manor, and might have interfered, or claimed ground-rent, but in a former generation much careless good-nature existed among landlords, and squatters were suffered to

seize on and appropriate land that was regarded of trifling value. The former Lord
Lamerton perhaps knew nothing of the ap-
propriation. His agent was an old, gouty,
easy-going man who looked into no matters
closely, and so the Saltrens became possessed
of Chillacot without having any title to show
for it. By the same process Patience Kite's
father had obtained his cottage, and Patience held her house on the same tenure
as Saltren held Chillacot. Usually when
settlers enclosed land and built houses, they
were charged a trifling ground-rent, and they
held their houses and fields for a term of
years or for lives, and the holders were
bound to keep the dwellings in good repair.
But, practically, such houses are not kept up,
and when the leases expire, or the lives fall
in the houses fall in also. A landlord with such
dwellings and tenements on his property is
often glad to buy out the holders to terminate
the disgrace to the place of having in it so many
dilapidated and squalid habitations.

Saltren's house was not in a dilapidated
condition ; on the contrary, it was neat and

in excellent repair. Stephen drew a respectable salary as captain of the manganese mine and could afford to spend money on the little property of which he was proud. He had had the house recently re-roofed with slate instead of thatch, with which it had been formerly covered. The windows and doors had been originally made of home-grown deal, not thoroughly mature, and it had rotted. Saltren renewed the wood-work throughout. Moreover, the chimney having been erected of the same stone as that of Kite's cottage, had decayed in the same manner. Saltren had it taken down and rebuilt in brick, which came expensive, as brick had to be carted from fourteen miles off. But, as the captain said, one does not mind spending money on a job designed to be permanent. Saltren had restocked his garden with fruit trees three or four years ago, and these now gave promise of bearing.

The glen in which Chillacot lay was a "coombe," that is, it was a short lateral valley running up into hill or moor, and opening into the main valley through which flows the arterial stream of the district. It was a sequestered spot, and as the glen was narrow, it did not get its proper share of sun. Some said the glen was called Chillacoombe because it was chilly, but the rector derived the name from the Celtic word for wood.

We hear much now-a-days about hereditary instincts and proclivities, and a man's character is thought to be determined by those of his ancestors. But locality has much to do with the determination of character. Physical causes model, develop, or alter physical features ; national characteristics are so shaped, and why not individual characters also ?

The climate of England is responsible to a large extent for the formation of the representative John Bull. The blustering winds, the uncertain weather, go to the hardening of the Englishman's self-reliance, determination, and perseverance under difficulties. He cannot wait to make hay till the sun shines, he must make it whether the sun shines or not. Having to battle with wind and rain, and face the searching east wind, to confront sleet, and snow, and hail from childhood, when, with

shining face and satchel he goes to school,
the boy learns to put down his head and defy
the weather. Having learned to put down
his head and go along as a boy, he does the
same all through life, not against weather
only, but against everything that opposes,
with teeth clenched, and fists rolled up in his
breeches pocket.

The national characteristic affects the very
animals bred in our storm-battered isle. A
friend of the author had a puppy brought out
to him on the continent from England. That
little creature sought out, fought, and rolled
over every dog in the city where it was.

" Dat ish not a doug of dish countree ! "
said a native who observed its pugnacity.

" Oh, no, it is an English pup."

"Ach so ! I daught as much, it ist one
deevil ! "

Perhaps the gloom of Chillacot, its sunless-
ness, was one cause of the gravity that
affected Saltren's mind, and made him silent,
fanatical, shadow-haunted. The germs of the
temperament were in him from boyhood, but
were not fully developed till after his marri-

age and the disappointment and disillusioning that ensued. He was a man devoid of humour, a joke hurt and offended him, if it was not sinful, it closely fringed on sin, because he could not appreciate it. He had a tender, affectionate heart, full of soft places, and, but for his disappointment, would have been a kindly man ; but he had none to love. The wife had betrayed him, the child was not his own. The natural instincts of his heart became perverted, he waxed bitter, suspicious, and ready to take umbrage at trifles.

When Arminell came in front of the cottage, she saw Mrs. Saltren leaning over the gate. She was a woman who still bore the traces of her former beauty, her nose and lips were delicately moulded, and her eyes were still lovely, large and soft, somewhat sensuous in their softness. The face was not that of a woman of decided character, the mouth was weak. Her complexion was clear. Jingles had inherited his good looks from her. As Arminell approached, she curtsied, then opened the gate, and asked—

" Miss Inglett, if I may be so bold,

would so much like to have a word with you."

" Certainly," answered Arminell.

" Will you honour me, miss, by taking a seat on the bench?" asked Mrs. Saltren, pointing to a garden bench near the door.

Arminell declined graciously. She could not stay long, she had been detained already, and had transgressed the luncheon hour.

" Ah, Miss Inglett," said the captain's wife, " I did so admire and love your dear mother, the late lady, she was so good and kind, and she took—though I say it—a sort of fancy to me, and was uncommonly gracious to me."

" You were at the park once ? "

" I was there before I married, but that was just a few months before my lord married your mother, the first Lady Lamerton. I never was in the house with her, but she often came and saw me. That was a bad day for many of us—not only for you, miss, but for all of us—when she died. If she had lived, I don't think we could have fallen into this trouble."

" What trouble ? " Arminell asked. She

was touched by the reference to her mother, about whom she knew and was told so little.

"I mean, miss, the mine that is being stopped. Her dear late ladyship would never have allowed it."

"But it runs under the house."

"Oh, miss, nothing of the sort. That is what Mr. Macduff says, because he is trying to persuade his lordship to close the mine. It is not for me to speak against him, but he is much under the management of Mrs. Macduff, who is a very fine lady; and because the miners don't salute her, she gives Macduff no rest, day or night, till he gets his lordship to disperse the men. My lord listens to him, and does not see who is speaking through his lips. My brother James is a comical-minded man, and he said one day that Mr. Macduff was like the automaton chess-player that was once exhibited in London. Every one thought the wax doll played, but there was a young girl hid in a compartment under the table, and she directed all the movements of the chess-player."

"I really cannot interfere between my

lord and his agent, or intercept communications between Mr. Chess-player and Mrs. Prompter."

" Oh, no, miss ; I never meant anything of the sort. I was only thinking how different it would have been for us if my lady—I mean my late lady—were here. She was a good friend to us. Oh, miss, I shall never forget when I was ill of the typhus, and everyone was afraid to come near us, how my good lady came here, carrying a sheet to the window, and tapped, and gave it in, because she thought we might be short of linen for my bed. I've never forgot that. I keep that sheet to this day, and I shall not part with it ; it shall serve as my winding sheet. The dear good lady was so thoughtful for the poor. But times are changed. It is not for me to cast blame, or to say that my lady as now is, is not good, but there are different kinds of goodnesses as there are cabbage roses and Marshal Neils."

Arminell was interested and touched.

" You knew my dear mother well ? "

"I am but a humble person, and it is unbecoming of me to say it, though I have a brother who is a gentleman, who associates with the best in the land, and I am better born than you may suppose, seeing that I married a captain of a manganese mine. I beg pardon—I was saying that her ladyship almost made a friend of me, though I say it who ought not. Still, I had feelings and education above my station, and that perhaps led her to consult me when she came here to Orleigh and knew nothing of the place or of the people, and might have been imposed on, but for me. After I recovered of the scarlet fever——"

"I thought it was typhus?"

"It began scarlet and ended typhus. Those fevers, miss, as my brother James says in his droll way, are like tradesmen, they make jobs for each other, and hand on the patient."

"How long was that after Mr. Jingles—I mean your son, Mr. Giles Saltren, was born?"

"Oh,"—Mrs. Saltren looked about her

rather vaguely—" not over long. Will you
condescend to step indoors and see my little
parlour, where I think, miss, you have never
been yet, though it is scores and scores of
times your dear mother came there."

" I will come in," said Arminell readily.
Her heart warmed to the woman who had
been so valued by her mother.

The house was tidy, dismal indeed, and
small, but what made it most dismal was the
strain after grandeur, the gay table-cover,
the carpet with large pattern, the wall paper
black with huge bunches of red and white
roses on it, out of keeping with the dimensions of the room.

Arminell looked round and felt a rising
sense of the absurdity, the affectation, the
incongruity, that at any other moment would
have made her laugh inwardly, though too
well-bred to give external sign that she
ridiculed what she saw.

" Ah miss!" said Mrs. Saltren, " you're
looking at that beautiful book on the table.
My lady gave it me herself, and I value it,
not because of what it contains, nor for the

handsome binding, but because of her who gave it to me."

Arminell took up the book and opened it.

" But—" she said,—" the date. It is an annual, published three years after my mother's death."

" Oh, I beg your pardon, miss, I did not say my late lady gave it me. I said, my lady. I know how to distinguish between them. If it had been given me by your dear mother, who is gone, my late lady, do you suppose it would be lying here? I would not keep it in the room where I sit but rarely, but have it in my bed-chamber, where I could fold my hands over it when I pray."

" I should like," said Arminell, " to see the sheet that my poor dear mother gave you, and which you cherish so fondly, to wrap about you in the grave."

" With pleasure," said Mrs. Saltren. " No —I won't say with pleasure, for it calls up sad recollections, and yet, miss, there is pleasure in thinking of the goodness of that dear lady who is gone. Lor! miss, it did seem dreadful that my dear lady when on earth didn't take precedency over the daughter of an earl, but now, in heaven, she ranks above marchionesses."

Then she asked Arminell to take a chair, and went slowly upstairs to search for the sheet. While she was absent the girl looked round her, and now her lips curled with derision at the grotesque strain after refinement and luxury which were unattainable as a whole, and only reached in inharmonious scraps and disconnected patches.

This was the home of Jingles! What a change for him, from these mean surroundings, this tasteless affectation, to the stateliness and smoothness of life at Orleigh Park! How keenly he must feel the contrast when he returned home! Had her father dealt rightly by the young man, in giving him culture beyond his position? It is said that a man has sat in an oven whilst a chop has been done, and has eaten the chop, without being himself roasted, but then the temperature of the oven was gradually raised and gradually lowered. Young Saltren had jumped into the oven out of a cellar and passed every now and then back again to the latter. This alteration of temperatures would kill him.

Some time elapsed before Mrs. Saltren returned. She descended the stair slowly, sighing, with the sheet over her arm.

"You need not fear to catch the fever from it, miss," she said, "it has been washed many times since it was used—with my tears."

Arminell's heart was full. She took the sheet and looked at it. How good, how considerate her mother had been. And what a touch of real feeling this was in the faithful creature, to cherish the token of her mother's kindness.

The young are sentimental, and are incapable of distinguishing true feeling from false rhodomontade.

"Why!" exclaimed Arminell, "it has a mark in the corner S.S,—does not that stand for your husband's initials?"

The woman seemed a little taken aback, but soon recovered herself.

"It may be so. But it comes about like

this. I asked Stephen to mark the sheet for
me with a double L. for Louisa, Lady Lamerton, and a coronet over, but he was so
scrupulous, he said it might be supposed I had
carried it away from the park, and that as the
sheet was given to us, we'd have it marked as
our own. My husband is as particular about
his conscience as one must be with the bones
in a herring. It was Bond's marking ink he
used," said Mrs. Saltren, eager to give minute
circumstances that might serve as confirma-
tion of her story, "and there was a stretcher
of wood, a sort of hoop, that strained the linen
whilst it was being written on. If you have
any doubt, miss, about my story, you've only
to ask for a bottle of Bond's marking ink
and you will see that they have circular
stretchers—which is a proof that this is the
identical sheet my lady gave me. Besides,
there is a number under the letters."

" Yes, seven."

" That was my device. It rhymes with
heaven, where my lady,—I mean my late lady
is now taking precedence even of marchionesses."

Arminell said nothing.   The woman's mind was like her parlour, full of incongruities.

"Look about you, miss," continued Mrs. Saltren, "though I say it, who ought not, this is a pretty and comfortable house with a certain elegance which I have introduced into it.   My brother, James Welsh, is a gentleman, and writes a great deal.   You may understand how troubled my husband is at the thought of leaving it."

"But—why leave?"

"Because, Miss Inglett, he will have no work here.   He will be driven to go to America, and unfortunately he has expended his savings in doing up the house and planting the garden.   I am too delicate to risk the voyage, so I shall be separated from my husband.   My son Giles has already been taken from me."   Then she began to cry.

A pair of clove-pinks glowed in Arminell's cheeks.   She could hardly control her voice. These poor Saltrens were badly used; her father was to blame.   He was the occasion of their trouble.

"It must not be," said Arminell, starting up, "I will go at once and speak to his lordship."

CHAPTER VII.

A VISION.

WITHOUT another word Arminell left the cottage. As she did so, she passed Captain Saltren speaking to Captain Tubb. The former scarce touched his hat, but the latter saluted her with profound respect.

When she was out of hearing, Saltren, whose dark eyes had pursued her, said in a low vibrating tone—

"There she goes—one of the Gilded Clique."

" I think you might have shown her more respect, man," said Tubb. "Honour to whom honour is due, and she is honourable."

"Why should I show respect to her? If she were a poor girl earning her bread, I would salute her with true reverence, for God hath chosen the poor, rich in faith. But is it not written that it is easier for a camel to pass

through the eye of a needle, than for the rich
to enter into heaven ? "

" You've queer fancies, Cap'n."

" They are not fancies," answered Saltren ;
"as it is written, so I speak." Then he
hesitated. Something was working in his
mind, and for a moment he doubted whether
to speak it to one whom he did not regard as
of the elect.

But Saltren was not a man who could restrain himself under an over-mastering conviction, and he burst forth in a torrent of words,
and as he spoke his sombre eyes gleamed
with excitement, and sparks lit up and flashed
in them. Soft they usually were, and dreamy,
but now, all at once they kindled into
vehement life.

" I tell you, Tubb, the Lord hath spoken.
The last days are at hand. I read my Bible
and I read my newspaper, and I know that
the aristocracy are a scandal and a burden to
the country. Now the long-suffering of
heaven will not tarry. It has been revealed
to me that they are doomed to destruction."

" Revealed to *you !* "

"Yes, to me, an unworthy creature, as none know better than myself, full of errors and faults and blindness—and yet—to me. I was wrestling in spirit near the water's edge, thinking of these things, when, suddenly, I heard a voice from heaven calling me."

"How—by name? Did it call you Cap'n?"

Saltren hesitated. "I can't mind just now whether it said, Saltren, Saltren! or whether it said Mister, or whether Cap'n, or Stephen. I dare say I shall remember by-and-by when I come to turn it over in my mind. But all has come on me so freshly, so suddenly, that I am still dazed with the revelations."

"Go on," said Tubb, shaking his head dubiously.

"And when I looked up, I saw a book come flying down to me out of heaven, and I held up my hands to receive it, but it went by me into the water hard by where I was."

"Somebody chucked it at you," exclaimed the practical Tubb.

"I tell you, it came down out of heaven,"

said Saltren, impatiently. " You have no faith. I saw the book, and before I could lay hold of it, it went under the raft—I mean, it went down, down in the water, and I beheld it no more."

" What sort of a book was it ? "

" I saw it but for a moment, as it floated with the back upwards, before it disappeared. There was a head on it and a title. I could not make out whose head, but I read the title, and the title was clear."

" What was it ? "

" ' The Gilded Clique.' "

" Clique ! what was that ? "

" A society, a party, and I know what was meant."

" Some one must have chucked the book," again reasoned the prosaic Tubb.

" It was not chucked, it fell. I was wrong to tell you of my vision. The revelation is not for such as you. I will say no more."

" And pray, what do you make out of this queer tale ? " asked the captain of the lime quarry with ill-disguised incredulity.

" Is it not plain as the day ? I have had

revealed to me that the doom of the British aristocracy is pronounced, the House of Lords, the privileged class,—in a word, the whole Gilded Clique ? "

Tubb shook his head.

" You'll never satisfy me it weren't chucked," he said. " But, to change the subject, Saltren. You have read and studied more than I have. Can you tell me what sort of a plant Quinquagesima is, and whether it is grown from seed, or cuttings, or layers ? "

CHAPTER VIII.

ABREAST.

As Arminell left Chillacot she did not observe the scant courtesy shown her by Captain Saltren. She was brimming with sympathy for him in his trouble, with tender feeling for the wife who had so loved her mother, and for the son who was out of his proper element. It did not occur to her that possibly she might be regarded by Saltren with disfavour. She had not gone many paces from the house before she came on a middle-aged couple, walking in the sun, abreast, arm in arm, the man smoking a pipe, which he removed and concealed in the pocket of his old velvet shooting coat, when he saw Arminell, and then he respectfully removed his hat. The two had been at church. Arminell knew them by sight, but she had not spoken at any time to either. The man, she had heard, had once been a gamekeeper on the property, but had been dismissed, the reason forgotten, probably dishonesty. The woman was handsome, with bright complexion, and very clear, crystalline eyes, a boldly cut nose, and well curved lips. The cast of her features was strong, yet the expression of the face was timid, patient and pleading.

She had fair, very fair hair, hair that would imperceptibly become white, so that on a certain day, those who knew her would exclaim, " Why Joan ! who would have thought it ? Your hair is white." But some years must pass before the bleaching of Joan's head was accomplished. She was only forty, and was hale and strongly built.

She unlinked her arm from that of her companion and came curtseying to Arminell, who saw that she wore a hideous crude green kerchief, and in her bonnet, magenta bows.

" Do you want me ? " she asked coldly. The unæsthetic colours offended her.

" Please, my lady ! "

" I am not ' my lady.' "

Joan was abashed, and retreated a step.

"I am Miss Inglett. What do you want?"

"I was going to make so bold, my la— I mean, miss——." Joan became crimson with shame at so nearly transgressing again. "This is Samuel Ceely."

Arminell nodded. She was impatient, and wanted to be at home. She looked at the man whose pale eyes quivered.

"Is he your husband?" asked Arminell.

"No, miss, not exactly. Us have been keeping company twenty years—no more. How many years is it since us first took up wi' each other, Samuel?"

"Nigh on twenty-two. Twenty-two."

"Go along, Samuel, not so much as that. Well, miss, us knowed each other when Samuel was a desperate wicked (*i.e.* lively) chap. Then Samuel was keeper at the park. There was some misunderstanding. The head-keeper was to blame and laid it on Samuel. He's told me so scores o' times Then came his first accident. When was that, Samuel?"

"When I shooted my hand away? Nineteen years come next Michaelmas."

" Were you keeper, then ? " asked Arminell.

" No, miss, not exactly."

" Then, how came you with the gun ? "

" By accident, quite by accident."

Joan hastily interfered. It would not do to enquire too closely what he was doing on that occasion.

" When was your second accident, Samuel ? "

" Fifteen years agone."

" And what was that ? " asked Joan.

" I falled off a waggon."

Arminell interrupted. This was the scene of old Gobbo and young Gobbo re-enacted. It must be brought to an end. " Tell thou the tale," she said with an accent of impatience in her intonation, addressing Joan. " What is your name ? "

" Joan Melhuish, miss. Us have been sweethearts a great many years ; and, miss, the poor old man can't do a sight of work, because of his leg, and because of his hand. But, lor-a-mussy, miss, his sweepings is beautiful. You could eat your dinner, miss,

off a stable floor, where Samuel has swept.
Or the dog-kennels, miss,—if Samuel were
but with the dogs, he'd be as if in Paradise.
He do love dogs dearly, do Samuel. He's
that conscientious, miss, that if he was sound
asleep, and minded in his dream there was
a bit o' straw lying where he ought to ha'
swept clean, or that the dogs as needed it,
hadn't had brimstone put in their water, he'd
get up out o' the warmest bed—not, poor
chap, that he's got a good one to lie on—to
give the dog his brimstone, or pick up
thickey (that) straw."

She was so earnest, so sincere, that her
story appealed to Arminell's feelings. Was
the dust that the witch, Patience, had cast on
her head, taking effect and opening her eyes
to the sorrows and trials of the underground
folk?

"Please, miss! It ain't only sweeping he
does beautifully. If a dog has fleas, he'll
wash him and comb him—and, miss, he can
skin a hare or a rabbit beautiful—beautiful!
I don't mean to deny that Samuel takes time
about it," she assumed an apologetic tone,

" but then, miss, which be best, to be slow
and do a thing thorough, or be quick and
half do it ? Now, miss, what I was going
to make so bold as to say was, Samuel do be
a-complaining of the rheumatics. They've
a-took'n bad across the loins, and it be bad
for him out in all weathers weeding turnips,
and doing them odd and dirty jobs, men
won't do now, nor wimen n'other, what wi'
the advance of education, and the franchise,
and I did think it would be wonderful good
and kind o' you, miss, if you'd put in a word
for Samuel, just to have the sweeping o' the
back yard, or the pulling of rabbits, or the
cleaning up of dishes, he'd make a rare
kitchen-maid, and could scour the dogs as
well, and keep 'em from scratching over
much. Lord, miss ! what the old man do
want is nourishing food and dryth (dry air)
over and about him."

" I'll speak to the housekeeper—no, I will
speak to her ladyship about the matter. I have
no doubt something can be done for Samuel."

Joan curtsied, and her honest face shone
with satisfaction.

"Lord A'mighty bless you, miss! I have been that concerned about the old man—he is but fifty, but looks older, because of his two accidents. H's shy o' asking for hisself, because he was dismissed by the late lord; the upper keeper laid things on him he'd no right to. He's a man, miss, who don't set no store on his self, because he has lost a thumb and two fingers, and got a dislocated thigh. But there's more in Samuel than folks fancy, I ought to know best, us have kept company twenty years."

"Are you ever going to get married?"

Joan shook her head.

"But how is it," asked Arminell, "that you have not been married yet, after courting so long?"

"First the bursted gun spoiled the chance —but Lord, miss, though he's lost half his hand, he is as clever with what remains as most men with two."

"He was unable to work for his living, I suppose?"

"And next he were throwed down off a waggon, and he's been lame ever since. But,

Lord, miss! he do get along with the bad leg, beautiful, quite beautiful."

" You are not nearer your marriage than you were twenty years ago," said Arminell, pitifully.

" I have been that troubled for Samuel," said Joan, not replying, but continuing her own train of thought ; " I've feared he'd be took off to the union, and then the old man would ha' died, not having me to walk out with of a Sunday and bring him a little 'baccy. And I—I'd ha' nort in the world to live for, or to hoard my wages for, wi'out my old Samuel."

The woman paused, turned round and looked at the feeble, disabled wreck of a man, who put his crippled hand to his forelock and saluted.

" How came he to fall off the waggon ? " asked Arminell.

" Well, miss, it came of my being on the waggon," explained Ceely, " I couldn't have falled off otherwise."

" Were you asleep ? Was the waggon in motion ? "

Joan hastily interfered, it would not do for too close an enquiry to be made into how it came that Samuel was incapable of keeping himself firm on the waggon ; any more than it would do to go too narrowly into the occasion of his shooting off his hand.

" What was it, miss, you was a-saying ? Nearer our marriage ? That is as the Lord wills. But—miss—us two have set our heads on one thing. I don't mind telling you, as you're so kind as to promise you'd get Samuel a situation as kitchen-maid."

" I did not promise that ! "

' Well, miss, you said you'd speak about it, and I know well enough that what you speak about will be done."

" What is it you have set your heart on ? Can I help you to that ? "

" You, miss ! O no, only the Lord. You see, miss, I don't earn much, and Samuel next to nothing at all, so our ever having a home of our own do seem a long way off. But there's the north side of the church, where Samuel's two fingers and thumb be laid, us can go to them. And us have bespoke to the sexton the place whereabout the fingers and thumb lie. I ha' planted rosemary there, and know where it be, and no one else can be laid there, as his fingers and thumb be resting there. And when Samuel dies, or I die, whichever goes first is to lie beside the rosemary bush over his fingers and thumb, and when the t'other follows, Samuel or I will be laid beside the other, with only the fingers and thumb and rosemary bush between us,—'cos us ain't exactly married—and 'twouldn't be respectable wi'out. 'Twill be no great expense," she added apologetically.

When Joan Melhuish had told all her story, Arminell no longer saw the crude green kerchief and the magenta bows. She saw only the face of the poor woman, the crystal-clear eyes in which light came, and then moisture, and the trembling lips that told more by their tremor than by the words that passed over them, of the deep stirring in the humble, patient heart.

How often it is with us that, looking at others, who belong to an inferior, or only a

distinct class, we observe nothing but verdigris green kerchiefs and magenta bows, something out of taste, jarring with our refinement,
ridiculous from our point of view. Then we
talk of the whole class as supremely bar-
barous, grotesque and separate from us by
leagues of intervening culture, a class that
puts verdigris kerchiefs on and magenta
bows, as our forefathers before Christ painted
their bodies with woad. And we argue—
these people have no human instincts, no
tender emotions, no delicate feelings—how
can they have, wearing as they do green ties
and magenta bows ? Have the creatures
eyes ? Surely not when they wear such unæsthetic colours. Hands, organs, dimensions,
senses, affections, passions ? Not with
emerald-green kerchiefs. If we prick them
they do not bleed. If we tickle they cannot
laugh. If we poison them, they will not die.
If we wrong them—bah ! They wear
magenta bows and are ridiculous.

It needs, may be, a sod taken from their
soil, a little dust from their hearth shaken
over our heads to open our eyes to see that

they have like passions and weaknesses with ourselves.

Arminell, without speaking, turned to Samuel, and looked at him.

What was there in this poor creature to deserve such faithful love? He was a ruin, and not the ruin of a noble edifice, but of a commonplace man. There was no beauty in him, no indication of talent in his face, no power in the moulding of his brow. He looked absurd in his short, shabby, patched, velveteen coat, his breeches and gaiters on distorted limbs. His attitudes with the ill-set thigh were ungainly. And yet—this handsome woman had given up her life to him.

"He don't seem much to you, perhaps, miss," said Joan, who eagerly scanned Arminell's face, and with the instinctive jealousy of love discovered her thoughts. "But, miss, what saith the Scripture? Look not on his countenance, or on the height of his stature. You should ha' seen Samuel before his accidents. Then he was of a ruddy countenance, and goodly to look on. I always see him as he was."

She still searched Arminell's face for token of admiration.

"Lord, miss! tastes differ. Some like apples and others like onions. For my part, I do like a hand wi' two fingers on it, it is uncommon, it is properly out o' the way as hands are. And then, miss, Samuel do seem to me to ha' laid hold of eternity wi' two fingers and a thumb, having sent them on before him, and that is more than can be said of most of us poor sinners here below."

She still studied the girl's countenance, and Arminell controlled its expression.

"Then," Joan continued, "as for his walk, it is lovely. It is ever dancing as he goes along the road. It makes one feel young— a girl—to have his arm, there be such a lightness and swing in his walk."

"But—" Arminell began, then hesitated, and then went on with a rush, "are you not discontented, impatient, miserable?"

"Why so, miss?"

"Because you have loved him so long and see no chance of getting him."

" No, miss. If I get him here, I get him to give me only half a hand ; if I get him in the other world, I get his whole hand, thumb and two first fingers as well. I be content either way."

CHAPTER IX.

TANDEM.

On the edge of a moor, at the extreme
limits to which man had driven back savage
nature, where were the last boundary walls
of stone piled up without compacting mortar,
was a farm-house called Court. It stood at
the point where granite broke out from
under the schistose beds, and where it had
tilted these beds up into a perpendicular
position. A vast period of time had passed
since the molten granite thus broke forth, and
the ragged edges of upturned rock had been
weathered down to mere stumps, but on
these stumps sat the homestead and farm-
house of Court, with a growth of noble
sycamores about it.

A stream brawling down from the moor
swept half round this mass of old worn-down
rock, a couple of granite slabs had been cast
across it, meeting in the middle on a rude
pier, and this served as a foot-bridge, but

carts and waggons traversed the water, and
scrambled up a steep ascent cut out of the
rock by wheels and winter runs.

If Court had been a corn-growing farm,
this would have been inconvenient, but this,
Court was not. It was a sheep and cattle
rearing farm. and on it was tilled nothing
but a little rye and some turnips.

In an elastic air fresh from the ocean, at a
height of a thousand feet above the sea, the
lungs find delight in each inhalation, and the
pulses leap with perennial youth. Pecuniary
embarrassments cease to oppress, and the
political outlook appears less threatening.

At the bottom of yonder valley three
hundred feet above the sea-level, where a
steamy, dreamy atmosphere hangs, we see
that England is going to the dogs. the end of
English commerce, agriculture, the aristocracy, the church, the crown, the constitu-
tion is at hand—in a word, the *Saturday
Review* expresses exactly our temper of
mind. A little way up the hill, we think the
recuperative power of the British nation is so
great, the national vigour is so enormous,

that it will shake itself free of its troubles in time—in time, and with patience—in a word, we begin to see through the spectacles of the *Spectator*. But when we have our foot on the heather, and scent the incense of the gorse, and hear the stonechat and the pewit, and see the flicker of the silver cotton grass about us, why then—we feel we are in the best of worlds, and in the best little nook of the whole world, and that all mankind is pushing its way, like us, upward with a scramble over obstacles; it will, like us, in the end breathe the same sparkling air, and enjoy the same extensive outlook, and be like us without care.

From Court what a wonderful prospect was commanded. The Angel in the Apocalypse stood with one foot on the land, and the other in the sea; so Court stood half in the rich cultivated garden of the Western Paradise, and half in the utter desolation of treeless moor. To south and west lay woodlands and pasture, parks and villages, tufts of Scotch fir, cedars, oak and elm and beech, with rooks cawing and doves cooing, and the woodpecker hooting among them ; to the east and north lay the haunt of the blackcock and hawk and wimbrel, and tracts of heather flushed with flower, and gorse ablaze with sun, and aromatic as incense.

Far away in the north-west, when the sun went down, he set in a quiver of golf-leaf, he doubled his size, and expired like the phœnix in flame. That was when he touched the ocean, and in touching revealed it.

What a mystery there is in distance ! How the soul is drawn forth step by step over each rolling hill, down each half-disclosed valley. How it wonders at every sparkle where a far-off window reflects the sun, and admires where the mists gather in wooded clefts, and asks, what is that ? when the sun discloses white specks far away on slopes of turquoise ; as the Israelites asked when they saw the Manna. How a curling pillar of smoke stirs up interest, rising high and dispersing slowly. We watch and are filled with conjecture.

As the afternoon sun shines sideways on the moor-cheek, it discloses what it did not reveal at other times, the faintest trace of furrows where are no fields now, where no plough has run since the memory of man. Was corn once grown there? At that bleak altitude? Did the climate permit of its ripening at one time? No one can answer these questions, but how else account for these furrows occasionally, only under certain aspects discernible? And to Court there was a corn-chamber, a sort of tower standing on a solid basement of stone six feet above the ground, a square construction all of granite blocks, floored within with granite, and with a conical slated roof, and a flight of stone steps leading up to it. A tower—a fortress built against rats, who will gnaw through oak and even lead, but must break their teeth against granite.

The corn-chamber was overhung by a sycamore, and at its side a rown, or "witch-bean" as it is locally called—a mountain ash —had taken root, flourished and ripened its crimson berries.

On the lowest step but one of the flight leading to the corn-chamber sat Thomasine

Kite, the daughter of the white-witch, Patience.
The evening was still and balmy in the
valleys; here on the moor-edge airs ever
stirred and were crisp. The bells were ringing for evening service far away in a belfry
that stood on a hill against the western sky,
and their music came in wafts mingled with
the hum of the wind among the heather, and
the twitter among the sycamores.

Aloft, on the highest twig of the tallest
tree sat a crow calling itself in Greek, Korax!
and so pleased with the sound of its name in
Greek that it repeated its name again and
again, and grew giddy with vanity, and
nearly overbalanced itself, and had to spread
wings and recover its poise.

Thomasine was in a bad humour. All the
household of Court were away, master and
mistress, men and maids, and she was left
alone like that crow on the tree-tops.

" Tamsin !" muttered the girl, " what a
foolish name I have got. It's like damson, of
which they make cheese. If they'd call me by
my proper name of Thomasine, it would be
all right, but Tamsin I hate."

" Korax ! " croaked the crow. " Why was I not born in Greece to be called Korax ? Crow is vulgar."

"I'm tired of my place," grumbled the girl, " here I am a servant maid at Court, out of the world and hard worked. Nothing going on, nothing to see, no amusements, nothing to read."

Why was Thomasine restless and impatient for a change? She did not herself know. She was dissatisfied with what? She did not herself properly know. She had vigorous health ; she had work, but not more than what with her fresh youth and hearty body she could easily execute. She had sufficient to eat. The farmer and his wife were not exacting, nor rough and bad tempered. The workmen and women on the farm were, as workmen and women are, with good and bad points about them. Elsewhere she would meet with much the same sort of associates. She knew that. Her wage was not high, but it was as much as she was likely to get in a farm-house, and a small wage there with freedom was better than a

big wage in a gentleman's family with re
straint. She knew that. Yet she was not
content. She wanted something, and she
did not know what. She would give her
mistress notice and go elsewhere. Whither?
She did not know. At any rate it would be
elsewhere, a change ; and she craved for a
change, for she had been a twelvemonth in
one place. Would she like her new situation?
She did not know. Would she, when in a
town, look back on the healthy life at Court ?
Possibly ; she did not know. But she could
not stay, because as the passion for roving is
in the gipsy blood, so was the fever of unrest
in hers. She was tired of life as it presented
itself to her, uniform, commonplace, unsen-
sational.

There was a period in European history
when all was change, when every people
plucked itself out of its ancestral ground and
went a wandering ; when the whole of the
continent was trampled over by races gallop-
ing west, like cattle and wild beasts disturbed
by a prairie fire. What was the cause ? We
hardly know, but we know that there was not

a people, a race, a class which was not thus
inspired with the passion for change of
domicile. The Germans entitle that period
the time of the great Folk-wandering. We
are in the midst of such another Folk-
wandering, but it is not now the migration of
races and nations, but of classes and individuals ; the passion for change drives the
men and women out of the country to
towns, and the young out of their situations.
It is in the air, it is in their blood.

The evening sun touched the western sea,
and flared up in a spout of fire. Then
Thomasine rose to her feet. Her red hair
had fallen, and she bent her arms behind her,
to do it up. Gorgeous that hair was in the
evening sun, it seemed itself to be on fire, to
be incandescent in every hair, and her
attitude as she stood on the step was grand,
her vigorous, graceful form, her splendid
proportions were shown in perfection, with
bosom expanded, and her hands behind her
head collecting and tying and twisting the
fire that rained off it. The evening sun was
full on her, and filled her eyes that she could

see nothing ; but her handsome face was shown illuminated as a lamp against the cold grey walls of the corn-chamber. Her shadow was cast up the steps and against the door, a shadow that had no blackness in it, but the purple of the plum.

"Tamsin ! my word, you are on fire !"

She started, let go her hair, and it fell about her, enveloping her shoulders and arms in flame. Then she put one hand above her eyes, and looked to see who addressed her.

" You here, Archelaus ! What has brought you to this lost corner of the world, this time o' day ?"

" You, of course, Tamsin, what else ? "

" I wish you'd choose a better time than when I'm doing up my hair."

" I could not wish a better time than when you are in a blaze of glory."

The young man who spoke was Archelaus Tubb, son of the captain of the slate quarry. He was a simple, good-humoured, not clever young man. Strongly built, with sparkling eyes and a merry laugh, he was just such a fellow as would have made his way in the world, had he been endowed with wits. He was not absolutely stupid, but he was muddle-headed. He succeeded in nothing that he undertook. He had been apprenticed to a carpenter, and at the expiration of three years was unable even to make a gate.

He tried his hand at gardening, and dug graves for potatoes, and put in bulbs upside down. He had faculties, but was incapable of applying them, or was too careless to call them together and concentrate them on his work. There seemed small prospect of his earning wage above that of a day-labourer.

He had fair hair, an honest face, always on the alert for a laugh. As he had been unquali-fied for any trade, his father had given him work in the quarry, but therein he earned but a labourer's wage, fourteen shillings a week.

Thomasine reseated herself on the lowest step but one, and put her feet on the lowest, and crossed her hands on her lap.

"Arkie," said she; "I am going away from Court, the life here is too dull for me. I want to see the world."

"Where are you going, Tamsin?"

"Not to bury myself in a place where nothing is doing, again."

"Nothing doing! There is plenty of work on a farm."

"Work!" scorned Thomasine. "Who wants work now? not I—I want to go where there .are murders and burglaries and divorces—into a place where there is life."

"Queer sort of life that," said Archelaus, casting himself down on the lowest step.

"I want to be where those things are done and talked about," said Thomasine; "what do I care about how the corn looks, and whether the sheep have the foot-rot, and what per stone is the price of bullocks? Now—you need not sit on my feet."

"I will choose a higher step," said the lad; then he stepped past her, and seated himself on that above her.

"Upon my word, Tamsin," he said, "you have wonderful hair. It is like mother's copper kettle new scoured, and spun into spiders' threads. Some red hair," continued he, "is coarse as wire, but this," he put his fingers through the splendid waves, " but this——"

" Is not for you to meddle with," said Thomasine. " Shall I make my fortune with it in the world ? "

She stood up, and stepped past him, and seated herself on the step immediately above that he occupied.

" In the world ! " repeated Archelaus. " What world—that where murders and burglaries and divorces are the great subject of talk ? "

" Aye—in the world where something is doing, where there is life, not in the world of mangold-wurzel."

" I do not know, Tamsin," said the lad dispiritedly. " I hope not."

" Why not ? I am not happy here. I want to be where something is stirring. Why," said Thomasine with a flash of anger in her cheek and eye and the tone of her voice—" Why am I to be a poor farm girl, and Miss Arminell Inglett to have all she wishes ? She to be wealthy, and I to have nothing ? She to be happy, and I wretched ? I suppose I am good-looking, eh, Arkie?"

"Of course you are," said he, "but, Tamsin, I cannot talk to you as you are behind me."

"I do not care to see your face," said the girl, "the back of your collar and coat are enough for me. Is that your Sunday wide-awake?"

"Yes—what have you against it?"

"Only that there is a hole in it, there"— she thrust her finger through the gap in the crown, and touched his scalp.

"I know there is, Tamsin; a coal bounced on to it from the fire."

"Without bringing light to your brain."

"I shall change my place," said Archelaus; he stood up, stepped past the girl, and seated himself above her.

"Now," said he, "I can look down on, and seek for blemishes in your head."

"You will find none there—eh! Arkie? Shall I make my fortune with my hair? Coin it into gold and wear purple and fine linen, and fare sumptuously every day? That is what I want and will have, and I don't care how I get it ; so long as I get it. My head and hair are not for you."

Then she stood up, strode past Archelaus, and planted herself on the step higher than that he occupied.

" This is a queer keeping company, tandem fashion, and changing the leader," laughed Archelaus.

" We are not keeping company," answered Thomasine. " Tandem is best as we are, single best of all."

" I don't see why we should not keep company," said the lad.

" I do," answered Thomasine sharply, "have I not made it plain to you that I didn't want a life of drudgery, and that I choose to have a life in which I may amuse myself ? "

" Let us try to sit on the same step," said Archelaus, "and then we can discuss the matter together, better than as we are, with one turning the back on the other."

" There is not room, Arkie."

" I'll try it at all events," said he, as he got up and seated himself beside her. " Now we

are together, and can keep steady if one puts
an arm round the other."

" I will not be held by you," said she, and
mounted to the step above ; then she burst
out laughing, and pointed. " Do y' look
there," she said, " there is a keeping of company would suit you."

She indicated a pair that approached the
farm. The man was lame, with a bad hip,
and his right hand was furnished with two
fingers only—it was Samuel Ceely. His
maimed hand was thrust between the buttons
of his waistcoat, and on his right arm rested
the coarse red hand of Joan Melhuish.

"Do y' look there !" exclaimed Thomasine,
" are they not laughable ? They have been
courting these twenty years, and no nigher
marriage now than when they began ; it might
be the same with us, were I fool enough to
listen and wait for what you offer."

" It is no laughing matter," said the lad, " it
is sad."

" It is sad that she should be such a fool !
Will his fingers grow again, and his hip right
itself ? She should have looked about for

K

another lover twenty years ago. now it is too late, and I take warning from her. You, Arkie, are like Samuel Ceely, not in body but in wits, crippled and limping there."

"Tamsin!" exclaimed Arkie, "you shall not speak like that to me." He stood up and stepped to where she was, and seated himself again beside her. That was on the highest step, and they were now both with their backs to the granary door. He tried to take her hand.

" No, Arkie," she said, " I speak seriously, I will not be your sweetheart. I like you well enough. You are a good tempered, nice fellow, very good natured, and always cheerful, but I won't have you. I can't live on fourteen shillings a week, and I won't live in the country where there is nothing going on, but cows calving and turnips growing. There is no wickedness in either, and wickedness makes life various and enjoyable. I can read and write and cypher, and am tired of work accordingly. I want to enjoy myself. There is mistress!" she exclaimed, stood up, stepped aside, missed her footing, and fell to the bottom of the steps.

"Oh, Tamsin, if only you had let me hold you!" cried Archelaus, and ran down to raise her. "Then you would not have fallen." She had sprained her foot and could only limp.

CHAPTER X.

"SABINA GREEN."

IN the four-hundred-and-thirty-first number of the *Spectator* is a letter from Sabina Green, on the disordered appetite she had acquired by eating improper and innutritious food at school. "I had not been there above a Month, when being in the Kitchen, I saw some Oatmeal on the Dresser; I put two or three Corns in my Mouth, liked it, stole a Handful, went into my Chamber, chewed it, and for two Months after never failed taking Toll of every Pennyworth of Oatmeal that came into the House. But one Day playing with a Tobacco-pipe between my Teeth, it happened to break in my Mouth, and the spitting out the Pieces left such a delicious Roughness on my Tongue, that I could not be satisfied till I had champed up the remaining Part of the Pipe. I forsook the Oatmeal, and stuck to the Pipes three Months, in

which time I had disposed of thirty-seven
foul Pipes, all to the Boles. I left off eating
of Pipes and fell to licking of Chalk. Two
Months after this, I lived upon Thunderbolts, a certain long, round, bluish Stone,
which I found among the Gravel in our
Garden."

Arminell's mental appetite was as much
disordered as the physical appetite of Sabina
Green. Whether Gaboriau's novels bore
any analogy to the foul tobacco-pipes, we do
not pretend to say, their record of vice
certainly left an agreeable roughness on her
mental palate, but now without any inter-
mediate licking of chalk, she has clenched
her teeth upon a thunderbolt—a question
hard, insoluble, beyond her powers of masti-
cation. Besides, she was wholly unaware that
the thunderbolt had been laid in her path ex-
pressly that she might exercise her teeth
upon it.

A hundred and fifty years ago, Sabina
Green picked corns, licked chalk and
munched tobacco pipes, and the same thing
goes on nowadays. There are tens of thou-

sands of Sabina Greens with their mouths full, and with no appetite but for tobacco-pipes or thunderbolts. We have advanced—our pipes are now meerschaum—foam of the sea.

We have known young ladies who would touch nothing but meringues, and thereby seriously impair their constitutions and complexions. We have known others who could touch nothing but literary meringues, novels, and whose digestion revolted at solid food, but who crunched flummery romance at all times of day and night, till the flummery invaded their brains, filled their mouths, frothed in their hearts; and then tired of sweets they look out for what is pungent or foul—like the old tobacco-pipes.

An unwholesome trick into which German women fall is that of "naschen," of nibbling comfits and cakes all day long. They carry cornets of bonbons in their pockets, and have recourse to them every minute. They suffer much from disordered digestion, and fall into the green sickness, because they lack iron in the blood. How can they have iron in the

blood when they eat only sugar? Our
English girls have a similar infirmity, they
nibble at novels, pick at the unsubstantial, innutritious stuff that constitutes fiction all day
long. Do they lack iron in their moral
fibre? Are their souls bloodless and faint
with the green sickness? How can it be
other on a diet of flummery?

The stomach of the nibbler never hungers,
only craves; the appetite is supplanted by
nausea. The symptoms of disorder are permanent; languor of interest, debility of
principle, loss of energy in purpose, a disordered vision, and creeping moral paralysis.

If Arminell had reached the condition of
one of these novel-nibblers, what she had
heard would have produced no effect upon
her heart or brain because neither heart nor
brain would have been left in her. But she
had not been a habitual novel-reader, she had
read whatever came to hand, indiscriminately;
and the flummery of mere fiction would never
have satisfied her, because she possessed,
what the novel-nibblers do not possess, in-
telligence. No control had been exercised

over her reading, consequently she had read things that were unsuitable. She had a strong character, without having found outlets for her energy. A wise governess would have tested her, and then led her to pursuits which would have exerted her ambition and occupied her interest ; but her teachers had been either wedded to routine or intellectually her inferiors. Consequently she had no special interests, but that inner eagerness and fire which would impel her to take up and follow with enthusiasm any object which excited her interest. Her friends said of Arminell with unanimity that she was a disagreeable girl, but none said she was an empty-headed one.

On reaching the house, Arminell found that lunch was over, and that her father had gone out. He had sauntered forth, as the day was fine, to look at his cedars and pines in the plantations, and with his pocket-knife remove the lateral shoots. Lady Lamerton was taking a nap previous to the resumption of her self-imposed duties at Sunday-school.

Arminell was indisposed to go to school

and afternoon service in the church. After a solitary lunch she went upstairs to the part of the house where was Giles' school-room. She had not seen her brother that day, and as the little fellow was unwell, she thought it incumbent on her to visit him.

She found the tutor, Giles Inglett (*vulgo,* Jingles) Saltren, in the room with the boy. Little Giles had a Noah's Ark on the table, and was trying to make the animals stand on their infirm legs, in procession, headed by the dove which was as large as the dog, and half the size of the elephant.

Mr. Saltren sat by the window looking forth disconsolately. The child had a heavy cold, accompanied by some fever.

" If you wish to leave the school-room, Mr. Saltren," said Arminell, " I am prepared to occupy your place with the captive."

" I thank you, Miss Inglett," answered the tutor. " But I have strict orders to go through the devotional exercises with Giles this afternoon, the same as this morning."

" I will take them for you."

"You are most kind in offering, but having been set my tale of bricks to make without straw, I am not justified in sending another into the clayfield, in my room."

"I see—this is a house of bondage to you, Mr. Saltren. You hinted this morning that you meditated an *in exitu Israel de Egypto*."

The young man coloured.

"You tread too sharply on the heels of the *pied de la lettre*, Miss Inglett."

"But you feel this, though you shrink from the expression of your thoughts. You told me yourself this forenoon that you were not happy. If you leave us, whither do you propose going?"

"A journey in the wilderness for forty years."

"With what Land of Promise in view?"

"I have set none before me."

"None? I cannot credit that. Every man has his Land of Promise towards which he turns his face. Why leave the leeks and onions of Goshen, if you have but a stony desert in view as your pasture? I suppose the heart is a binnacle with its needle point-

ing to the pole—though each man may have
a different pole. South of the equator, the
needle points reversedly to what it pointed
north of it. An anchor, an iron link, a nail
even may divert the needle, but to something it must turn."

"Miss Inglett—had Moses any personal
hope to reach and establish himself in the land
flowing with milk and honey, when he led
Israel from the brick-kilns? He was to die
within sight of the land, and not to set foot
thereon."

"But, Mr. Saltren; who are your Israel?
Where are the brick-kilns? Who are the
oppressors?"

"Can you ask?" The tutor paused and
looked at the girl. "But I suppose you
fail to see that the whole of the civilised
world is an Egypt, in which some are task-
masters and others slaves ; some enjoy and
others suffer. Miss Inglett—you have
somehow invited my confidence, and I
cannot withhold it. It is quite impossible
that the world can go on as it has been,
with one class drawing to itself all that life

has to offer of happiness, and another class doomed to toil and hunger and sweat, and have nothing of the light and laughter of life."

Arminell seated herself.

"Well," she said, "as Giles is playing with his wooden animals, trotting out the contents of his ark; let us turn out some of the strange creatures that are stuffed in our skulls, and marshal them. I have been opening the window of my ark to-day, and sending forth enquiries, but not a blade of olive has been brought to me."

"As for the ark of my head," said the tutor with a bitter smile, "it is the reverse of that of Noah. He sent forth raven and dove, and the dove returned, but the raven remained abroad. With me, the dark thoughts fly over the flood and come home to roost; the dove-like ones—never."

"I am rather disposed," said Arminell, laughing, "to liken my head to a rookery in May. The matured thoughts are a-wing and wheeling, and the just fledged ones stand cawing at the edge of their nests, with fluttering wings, afraid to fly, and afraid to stay and be shot."

" To be shot ?—by whom ?"

" Perhaps, by your wit. Perhaps by my lord's blunderbuss."

" I will not level any of my poor wit at them. Let your thoughts hop forth boldly that I may have a sight of them."

An exclamation of distress from Giles.

" What is the matter ?" asked Arminell, turning to her brother.

" The giraffe has broken his leg, and I want him to stand because he has such a long neck."

" If you were manly, Giles, you would not say, the giraffe has broken his leg, but—I have broken the giraffe's leg."

" But I did not, Armie. He had been packed too tightly with the other beasts, and his leg was so bent that it broke."

" Mend it with glue," she advised.

" I can't—it is wrong to melt glue on Sunday. Mamma would not like it."

The conversation had been broken along with the giraffe's leg, and neither Arminell

nor young Saltren resumed it for some time,
Presently the girl said, "Mr Saltren, do you
know what sort of men Addison called
Fribblers? They are among men what flirts
are among women, drawing girls on and then
disappointing them. There are plenty of
flirts and fribblers in other matters. There
are flirts and fribblers with great social and
religious questions, who play with them, trifle
with them, hover about them, simulate a lively
interest in them, and then—when you expect
of them a decision and action on that decision,
away they fly in another direction, and shake
all interest and inquiry out of their thoughts.
I have no patience with such flirts or fribblers." She spoke with a little bitterness.
She was thinking of her step-mother. The
tutor knew it, but did not allow her to see
that he did.

"Do you not think," he said, "that they
fribble from a sense of incompetence to grapple
with these questions? The problems interest
them up to a certain point. Then they see
that they are too large for them, or they entail
consequences they shrink from accepting, con-

sequences that will cost them too dear, and they withdraw."

" Like the young man in the Gospel who went away sorrowful for he had great possessions. He was a fribbler."

" Exactly. He was a fribbler. He was insincere and unheroic."

" I could not fribble," said Arminell vehemently. " If I see that a cause is right, I must pursue it at whatsoever consequence to myself. It is of the essence of humdrum to fribble. Do you know, Mr. Saltren, I have had a puzzling problem set before me to-day, and I shall have no rest till I have worked it out? Why is there so much wretchedness, so much inequality in the world ?"

" Why was Giles' giraffe's leg broken ? "

Arminell looked at him with surprise, suspecting that instead of answering her, he was about to turn off the subject with a joke.

" The world," said Saltren, " is like Giles' Noah's Ark, packed full—over full—of creatures of all kinds, and packed so badly that they impinge on, bruise, and break each other. Not only is the giraffe's leg broken,

but so are the rim of Noah's hat and the ear
of the sheep, and the tusk of the elephant   It
is a congeries of cripples.   We may change
their order, and we only make fresh abrasions.
The proboscis of the elephant runs into the
side of the lamb, and Noah's hat has been
knocked of by the tail of the raven.   However you may assort the beasts, however
carefully you may pack them, you cannot prevent their doing each other damage."

Mr. Saltren turned to little Giles and
said :—

" Bring us your box of bricks, my boy."

" It is Sunday," answered the child.
" Mamma would not wish me to play with
them."

" I do not wish to make a Sabbath-breaker
of you," answered the tutor, " nor are your
sister and I going to do other than build Babel
with them—which is permissible of a Sunday."

The little boy slid off his seat, went to his
cupboard, and speedily produced the required
box, which he gave to Mr. Saltren.

The tutor drew forth the lid.   The bricks
were all in place compacted in perfect order.

Then he said, with half-sneer, half-laugh, " There are no gaps between them. The whole assemblage firm as it were one block. Not a breakage anywhere, not room for a breakage."

" No," said Arminell, " of course not. They all fit exactly because they are all cubes. The bricks," she laughed, "have no long necks like the giraffe, or legs or horns, or proboscis, or broad-brimmed hats, liable to be broken. Of course they fit together."

" If you shake the ark—the least concussion produces a breakage, one or two beasts suffer. You may toss the box of bricks about ; and nothing is hurt. Why ? "

Arminell was impatient. " Of course the reason is plain."

" The reason is plain. *The bricks are all equal.* If it were so in the world of men, there would be no jars, no fractures, no abrasions, but concord, compactness, peace."

Arminell said nothing. She closed her eyes and sat looking at the bricks, then at the animals Giles had arranged.

The tutor said no more, but his eyes, bright and eager, were on the girl's face.

Presently Arminell had gathered her thoughts together sufficiently to speak.

"That, then, is the solution you offer to my problem. But to me it does not seem solved. There the animals are. They are animals—and not bricks."

"They are animals, true, but they must be shaken and shaken together, till all their excrescences are rubbed away, and then they will fit together and find sufficiency of room. That is how marbles are made. Shapeless masses of stone are put in a bag and rattled till all their edges and angles are rattled off."

"What an ark would remain! You complain of some animals crippling others, this scheme of yours would involve a universal mutilation—the animals resolved into undistinguishable, shapeless, uninteresting trunks. The only creature that would come out scatheless would be the slug. All the rest would be levelled down to the condition of that creature—which is a digesting tube, and nothing more." Then Arminell

stood up. " It is time for me to be off," she
said ; " her ladyship will be back from
church, and oh ! Mr. Saltren, I have interfered with the Psalms and Lessons."

CHAPTER XI.

ACCORDING to the classic story, the Sphinx demanded of all who visited her the solution of an enigma—and that enigma was *Man.*

Suddenly, unexpectedly, on a quiet ordinary Sunday morning, Arminell, a young girl without experience, had been confronted with the Sphinx, and set the same enigma, an enigma involving others, like the perforated Chinese puzzle-balls, an enigma that has been essayed and answered repeatedly, yet always remains insoluble, that, as it has assumed fresh aspects, has developed new perplexities. Arminell had been wearied with the routine and restraint of social life, its commonplace duties and conventionalities, and had been fired with that generous though mistaken dislike to the insincerities and formalities of civilisation, so often found among the young—generous, because bred of

truth ; mistaken, because it ignores the fact
that the insincerities impose on no one, and
the formalities are made of mutual com-
promises, such as render life, social life,
possible.

Arminell was in this rebellious mood,
when she was brought face to face with a
problem beyond her powers to unravel.
She might as well, with a rudimentary knowledge of algebraic symbols, have been set to
work out Euler's proof of the Binomial
Theorem. She was like Fatima when she
opened Blue-Beard's secret chamber, and
saw in it an array of victims. Of these
victims disclosed to her, one was Jingles,
another Patience Kite ; then came Captain
Saltren and his wife ; and next hung in the
dismal cabinet of horrors, Samuel Ceely and
Joan Melhuish. The world was indeed a
Blue-Beard's room. If you but turned the
key you saw an array of misery and tearful
faces, and hearts with blood distilling from
them. It was more than that—it was a box
with a Jack in it. She had touched the
spring, and a monster had flown up in her

face, not to be compressed and buttoned down again.

How could the facts of existence be reconciled with the idea of Divine Justice? On one side were men and women born to wealth and position and happiness; on the other, men and women denied the least of the blessings of life. Why were some of God's creatures petted and pampered, and others kicked about and maltreated? Was the world of men so made from the beginning, or had things so come about through man's mismanagement, and if so, where was the over-ruling Providence which governed the world? When the Noah's Ark arrived new from the great toy-shop whence issue the planets and spheres, were all the figures round and fitted together, only afterwards in the rearrangement to impinge on and mutilate each other? Or had they been all alike in the beginning and had developed their horns and proboscises, their tusks and broad-brimmed hats? Life is a sort of pantomime, that begins with a fairy tale, leads to a transformation scene, and ends, perhaps, with low comedy. In a moment when we least expect it, ensues a blaze of light, a spectacular arrangement of performers, and then, away fall the trappings of splendour, and forth, from under them, leap out harlequin, clown, and pantaloon. The knights cast off their silver armour, the fairies shed their gauzy wings, kings and queens depose their crowns and sceptres, and there are revealed to us ordinary men and women, with streaks of paint on their faces, and patches of powder in their hair, perpetrating dismal jokes, the point of which we fancy is levelled at ourselves.

To some men and women the transformation scene arrives late in life, but to all inevitably at some time ; and then when the scene on the stage before us is changed, a greater transformation ensues within.

When we were children we believed that everything glittering was gold, that men were disinterested and women sincere. The transformation scene came on us, perhaps with coruscations of light and grouping of colours and actors, perhaps without, and went by, leaving us mistrustful of every person, doubtful of everything, sceptical, cynical, disenchanted. Is not—to take a crucial case—marriage itself a grand transformation scene that closes the idyl of youth, and opens the drama of middle age? We live for a while in a fairy world, the flowers blaze with the most brilliant colours, the air is spiced as the breezes of Ceylon, angels converse with men, and sing æthereal music, manna floats down from heaven, containing in itself all sweetness; sun and moon stand still o'er us, over against each other, not to witness a conflict, as of old in Ajalon, but to brighten and prolong the day of glamour. Then the bride appears before us, as Eve appeared to Adam, unutterably beautiful and perfect and innocent, and we kneel in a rapture, and dare not breathe, dare not speak, nor stir; and swoon in an ecstasy of wonder and adoration.

Then tingle the marriage bells. The transformation scene is well set with bridesmaids and orange-blossoms, and a wedding breakfast, postboys with favours, and a shower of rice, and then—?

The fairy tale is over. The first part of the pantomime is over. The colours have lost their brilliancy, the flowers shrivel, the scents are resolved into smells of everyday life, broiled bacon, cabbage water, and the light is eclipsed as by a November fog. The men for the way-rate, the water-rate, and the gas-rate are urgent to have a word with us. There descend on our table at every quarter most bitter bills—those of the butcher and the green-grocer, the milliner's little account, and the heavy itemless bill from the doctor. What shall we say about our Eve, the beautiful, the all-but divine, the ideal woman? The all-but divine turns out to have a touchy temper and a twanging tongue, falls out with her cook, dismisses her, and consequently serves you cold mutton and underboiled potatoes.

The transformation is complete, and how does it leave us? In a rage at our folly? Cursing our idealism? Rasped and irritable? Withdrawing more and more from the society of our Eve, and our Eden turned to an es- palier garden, to our club? So it is in many cases. The transformation scene is a trial, and certain ones there are that never recover the shock of disenchantment; but there are others, on the other hand, who endure, and to them comes in the end a reward. These continue to sit in their box, listless, paring their nails, turning the programme face downwards. Half contemptuously, wholly void of interest, they lend a dull ear to what follows, and look on with a wondering eye, convinced that the rest is farce and buffoonery and a vexation of spirit, which must however be sat through; then, little by little fresh interests arise, tiny new actors invade the stage, with sweet but feeble voices, saying nothing of point, yet full of poetry. The magic begins to work once more, the little fingers weave a spell that lays hold of heart and brain, and conjures up a new world of fantasy. The flowers re-open and flush with colour, the balmy air fans our jaded faces, again the songs of angels reach our ears, the clouds dispel, the manna falls, Eve resumes her beauty, not the old beauty of childlike innocence and freshness, but that of ripened womanhood, of sweet maternity, of self-command and self-devotion.

We sit hushed with our head in our hands, and look with intense eye, and listen with sharpened ear, and the tears rise and run down our cheeks. We have forgotten the old Eden with its fantastic imaginations, in the more matured, the richer, the fuller, and above all the more real paradise that is now revealed.

In the case of Arminell Inglett there was no enchantment of colour, no setting of tableau, for the transformation scene; it came on her suddenly but also quietly. In one day, on a quiet country Sunday, when she walked out of the dull and stuffy school, she passed, as it were, through a veil, out of childland into the realm of Sphinx.

In the evening, after a dull dinner, instead of remaining in the drawing-room with my lady, who had taken up a magazine, Arminell put a shawl over her head and shoulders, went forth into the garden, and thence to the avenue.

The evening was pleasantly warm, the

weather beautiful ; beneath the trees the dew
did not fall heavily.   A new moon was shining.   The girl thought over what she had
heard and seen that day—over the troubles
and wrongs of Captain Saltren, driven from
his occupation, and yet chained to the house
that was his own, and with which he would
not part ; over the defiant scepticism of
Patience Kite, at war in heart with God and
man ; over the suffering lives of Samuel and
Joan, united in heart, yet severed by fate, looking to a common grave as the marriage bed,
and Arminell felt almost contempt for these
latter, because they accepted their lot without
resentment.   She thought over what young
Mr. Saltren had said about his own position,
and she was able to understand that it was
one of difficulty and discomfort.

Then she turned her mind to the Sunday-
school, where, whilst outside of it, within the
narrow confines of Orleigh parish, there was
so much of trouble and perplexity, my lady
was placidly teaching the children to recite as
parrots the names of the books of the
Apocrypha, which they were not to read for the

establishment of doctrine, and Captain Tubb
was enunciating arrant nonsense about the
names of the Sundays preceding Lent.

The avenue was composed of ancient oaks.
It was reached from the garden, which inter-
vened between the house and it.   The avenue
was not perfectly in line, because the lay of
the land did not admit of its being carried at
great length without a curve, following the
slope of the hill that rose above it, and fell
away below in park-land to the river.

The walk was gravelled with white spar.
It commanded an exquisite view down the
valley of the Ore, over rich meadow-land and
pasture, dotted with clumps of trees, beech,
chestnut, and Scotch pine.   A line of alders
marked the course of the river, to where, by
means of a dam, it had been widened into a
lake.   On the further side of the river, the
ground gently rose in grassy sweeps to the
wooded hills.   To the south-west the river
wound away about shoulders of richly-clothed
hills, closing in on each other, fold on fold.
The avenue was most delightful in the evening when the setting sun gilded the valley

with its slant beams, turned the trunks of the pines scarlet, and cast the shadows of the park trees a purple blue on the illuminated grass.

Oaks do not readily accommodate themselves to form avenues, they are contorted, gnarled, consequently oak avenues are rarely met with. That at Orleigh had the charm of being uncommon.

The evening was still, the sky was full of light, so much so that the stars hardly showed. The light spread as a veil from the north, from behind the Orleigh woods, and reflected itself in the dew that bathed the grass. Arminell was attached to this walk, in great measure because she could at almost all times saunter in it undisturbed.

She had not, however, on this occasion, been in it half an hour, before she saw her father coming to her. He had left his wine ; there were, as it happened, no guests in the house, and he and the tutor had not many topics in common.

"Well, Armie !" he said, " I have come out to have a cigar, and lean on you. My lady told me I should find you here."

" And, papa, I am so glad you have come, for I want to have a word with you."

" About what, child ? " Lord Lamerton was a direct man—a man in his position must be direct to get through all the business that falls to him, business which he cannot escape from, however much he may desire it.

" Papa," said Arminell, " it is about the Saltrens."

" What about them ? "

" If you give up the manganese—what is Captain Saltren to do ? "

" Stephen will find work somewhere, never fear."

" But he cannot leave his house."

" That he will have to sell ; the railway company want to cross Chillacombe at that point. He will get a good price, far beyond the value of the house and plot of land."

" Papa—must the manganese be given up ? "

" Of course it must. I have no intention of allowing myself to be undermined."

" But it is so cruel to the men who worked on it."

"Manganese no longer pays for working. There has been a loss on the mine for the last five years. We are driven out of the market by the Eiffel manganese. The Germans work at less wage, and our men refuse to have their wage reduced."

"But what are the miners to do?"

"They were given warning that the mine would be closed, as long as five years ago; and the warning has been renewed every year since. They have known that they must seek employment elsewhere. They will have to go after work, work will not come to them—it is the same in every trade. All businesses are liable to fluctuations, some to extinction. When the detonating cap was invented, the old trade of flint chipping on the Sussex downs began to languish; with the discovery of the lucifer match it expired altogether. When adhesive envelopes were introduced, the wafer-makers and sealing-wax makers were thrown out of work, and the former trade was killed outright. I was wont to harvest oak-bark annually, and put many hundreds of pounds in my pocket. Now the

Americans have superseded tan by some chemical composition, and there is no further sale for bark. I am so many hundreds of pounds the poorer."

" Yes, papa, that is true enough, but you have a resisting power in you that others have not. You have your rents and other sources of income to fall back on ; these poor tradesmen and miners and artizans have none. I have read that in Manitoba the secret of the magnificent corn crops is found in this, that the ground is frozen in winter many feet deep, and remains frozen in the depths all summer, but gradually thaws and sends up from below the released water to nourish the roots of the wheat, which are thus fed by an unfailing subterranean fountain. It is so with you, you are always heavy in purse and flush in pocket, because you also have your sources always oozing up under your roots."

" My dear Armie, my subterranean source —the manganese—is exhausted ; for five years instead of being a source it has been a sink."

" Whereas," continued Arminell, " the poor and the artizan lie on shelfy rock, with

M

shallow soil above it.   A drought—a week of
sun—and they are parched up and perish."

"My dear girl, the analogy is false.   The
difference between us is between the rooted
and the movable creature.   Do not they live
on us, eat us   consume our superfluity ?
We are vegetables—that root in the soil,
and the tradesmen and artizans nibble and
browse on us.   The richer our leaf, the more
succulent our juices, the more nutriment we
supply to them.   When they have eaten us
down to the soil, they move off to other
pastures and nibble and browse there.
When we have recovered, and send up fresh
shoots, back they come, munch, munch,
munch.   If one supply fails, others open.
There is equipoise—I dare say there are
twice as many hands employed in making
matches and adhesive envelopes now, as
there were of old chipping flints and making
wafers."

"That may be, but the drying up of one
spring before another opens must cause distress.   Where is that other one, that the
necessitous may drink of it ?   Ishmael was

dying of thirst in the desert on his mother
Hagar's lap, within a stone's throw of a well
of which neither knew till it was shown them
by an angel."

" Of course there is momentary distress,
but the means of locomotion are now so
great that every man can go about in quest
of work. Things always right themselves in
the end."

" They do not right themselves without the
crushing and killing of some in the process.
Tell me, papa, how is this to be explained?
I have to-day encountered two poor creatures
who have loved each other for twenty years,
and are too abject in their poverty to be able
even now to marry. No fault of either
accounts for this. Accident, misfortune,
divide them—such things ought not to be."

" But they are—they cannot be helped."

" They ought not to be—there must be
fault somewhere. Either Providence in
ruling destinies rules them crooked, or the
social arrangements brought about by
civilization are to blame."

" Here, Armie, I cannot follow you. I

am content with the providential ordering of the world."

"Of course you are, papa, on fifty thousand a year."

"You interrupt me. I say I am content with the social structure as built up by civilization."

"I have no doubt about it—you are a peer. But what I want to know is, how do the providential and social arrangements look to the Fredericks with the Empty Pockets, not what aspect they wear to Maximilian and Le Grand Monarque. Do you suppose that Captain Saltren is content that his livelihood should be snatched from him ; or Patience Kite that her father and mother should have died, leaving her in infancy a waif ; or Samuel Ceely, that he should have blown off his hand and blown away his life's happiness with it, and dislocated his hip and put his fortunes for ever out of joint thereby, so as to be for ever incapacitated from making himself a home, and having a wife and little children to cling about his neck and call him father ? "

" Old Sam was not all he ought to have been before he met with his accidents."

" Nor are any of us all we ought to be. Papa, why should it have fallen to your lot to have two wives, and Samuel Ceely be denied even one ? "

" Upon my word, Armie, I cannot tell."

" I do not suppose you can see how those are who live on the north side of the hill always in shade and covered with mildew, when you bask on the south side always in sun, where the strawberries ripen early, and the roses bloom to Christmas."

" I beg your pardon, child, I have had my privations. We cannot afford to go to town this season. I have had to make a reduction in my rents of twenty per cent. I get nothing from my Irish property, cannot sell my bark, lose by my manganese. Are you satisfied ? "

" No, papa, your privations are loss of luxuries, not of necessaries. Those who have been exposed to buffets of fortune, been scourged by the cynical and cruel caprice which rules civilized life, will rise up and exact their portions of life's pleasures and comforts. They will say,—we will not be exposed to the chance of being full to-day and empty to-morrow, of working without hope—like Samuel and Joan."

" Sam does not work."

" That is the fault of Providence which blew off his hand and distorted his leg. I say, the needy and the workers will ask why we should be well-dressed, well-housed, well-fed, hear good music, buy good pictures, ride good horses——" her thoughts moved faster than her words ; she broke off her sentence without finishing it. " Papa ! why, at a meet, should Giles have his pony and little Cribbage run on his feet ? "

" Upon my soul," answered Lord Lamerton, " I can't answer in any other way than this—because I keep a pony and the rector does not for his little boy."

" But, papa, I think the time must come when you will have to justify your riding a good hunter and wearing a red coat ; and I for wearing a tailor-made habit, whilst Miss Jones has but a skirt."

" Look here, Armie," said her father, " how
dense, how like snow the fog is lying on the
pasture by the water."

" Yes, papa, but——"

" There is no fog here, on the higher
land."

" No, papa."

" There is frost below when there is none
here."

" Yes, papa."

" Why so ?"

" Because that lies low, and this high."

" But why should that lie low, and this
high ?"

" Of course, because—it is the configuration of the land."

" But how unreasonable, how unjust, that
there should be such configuration of the
land, as you call it. There should be no
elevations and no depressions anywhere—a
universal flat is the landscape for you."

Arminell winced. She saw the drift of
her father's remarks.

' My dear," he said, " there must be inequalities in the social level, but I am not

sure that these very inequalities do not give
charm and richness to the social picture.
Each level has its special flora. The mari-
gold and the milkmaid and the forget-me-
not love the low moist bottom where the
fog and frost hang, and will not thrive here.
Those ups and downs, those hills and valleys
which so shock your sense of fitness, are the
secret of richness, are the secret of fertility.
In equatorial Africa, Dr. Schweinfurth found
a dead level and perennial swamp. In Mid-
Asia, Huc traversed an Alpine plateau
absolutely sterile. It is a very unreasonable
thing to some that our moors should contain so
many acres of unprofitable bog, that they
should be sponges receiving, and growing
nothing. They say that we, the wealthy,
are these absorbing sponges, unprofitable
bogs of capital. But, my dear child, if the bogs
were all drained, all the water would run off
as fast as it fell. They retain the water and
gradually discharge it on the thirsty lowlands.
And so is it with us. We spend what we receive and enrich therewith those beneath.
But come—I shall go in. I am feeling chilled."

"I will take another turn first," said Arminell.

"Don't fret yourself, my dear," said her father, "about these matters. Take the world as it is."

"Papa—-that advice comes too late. I cannot "

CHAPTER XII.

SINTRAM.

Lord Lamerton returned to the house; he threw away his cigar-end, and went in at the snuggery door, the door into the room whither the gentlemen retired for pipes and spirits and soda-water, a room ornamented with foxes' heads and brushes, whips, hunting-pictures, and odds and ends of all sorts. He shut the door and passed through it into that part of the house in which was the school-room, and Giles' sleeping apartment. As he entered the passage, Lord Lamerton heard piercing shrieks, as from a child yelling in terror or pain.

In a moment, Lord Lamerton ran up the stairs towards the bedroom of his son. The nurse was there already, with a light, and was sitting on the bed, endeavouring to pacify the child. Giles sat up in his night-shirt, in the bed clothes, with his eyes wide open, his fair head disordered, striking out with his hands in recurring paroxysms of terror.

"What is the matter with him?" asked the father.

"My lord—he has been dreaming. He has had one or two of these fits before. Perhaps his fever and cold have had to do with it." Then hastily to Giles who began to kick and beat, and went into a fresh fit of cries, "There, there, my dear, your papa has come to see you. Have you nothing to say to him?"

But the little boy was not to be quieted. He was either still asleep, or, if awake, he saw something that bereft him of the power of regarding anything else.

"There will be no questioning him, my lord, till he is thoroughly roused," said the nurse.

"Bring me a glass of water."

Whilst the woman went for the tumbler, Lord Lamerton seated himself on the bedside, and drew the little boy up, and seated him on his lap.

"Giles, my darling, what is the matter ?"

Then the little fellow clung round his father's neck, and the tears broke from his eyes, and he began to sob.

"What is the matter, my pet, tell me? Have you had bad dreams? Here, drink this draught of cold water."

"No, no, take it away," said the child. "I want papa to stay. Papa, you won't be taken off, will you ? Papa, you will not leave me, will you ?"

"No, my dear. What have you been thinking about ?"

"I have not been thinking. I saw it."

"Saw what, Giles ?"

Lord Lamerton stroked the boy's hair ; it was wet with perspiration, and now his cheeks were overflowed with tears. The shrieks had ceased. He had recovered sufficient consciousness to control himself ; "Papa, I was at the window."

"What, in your night-shirt ? After you had been put to bed? That was wrong. With your heavy cold you should not have left your bed."

The child seemed puzzled.

" Papa, I do not understand how it was. I would not have left bed for the world, if I thought you did not wish it ; and I do not remember getting out—still, I must have got out ; for I was at the window."

" He has not left his bed. He has been dreaming, my lord," explained the nurse in an undertone ; and Lord Lamerton nodded.

" Papa, dear."

" Yes, my pet."

" Are you listening to me ? "

" I am all attention."

" Papa, I was at the window. But I am very sorry that I was there, if you are annoyed. I will not do it again, dear papa. And the moon was shining brightly on the drive. You know how white the gravel is. It was very white with the moon on it. I did not feel at all cold, papa ; feel me, I am quite warm."

"Yes, my treasure, go on with your story."

" Then I watched something black come all the way up the drive, from the lodge-gates, through the park. I could not at first

make out what it was, but I saw that it was
something very, very black, and it came on
slowly like a great beetle. But when it was
near, then I saw it was a coach drawn by four
black horses, and there was a man on the box,
driving, and he was in black. There was no
silver nor brass mounting to the harness of
the horses, or I should have seen it sparkle
in the moonlight. And, dear papa, the coach
stole on without making any noise. I saw
the horses trotting, and the wheels of the
coach turning, but there was no sound at all
on the gravel. Was not that strange ?"

"Very strange indeed, my dear."

" But there was something much stranger.
I saw that the horses had no heads, and also
that the coachman had no head. His hat
with the long weeper was on the top of the
carriage. He could not wear it because he
was without a head. Was not that queer ?"

" Very queer," answered Lord Lamerton,
and signed to the nurse to leave the room.
His face looked grave, and he held the little
boy to his heart, and kissed his forehead with
lips that somewhat quivered.

" Then, papa, the carriage stopped at the entrance, and I could see through the window panes to the gravel with the moon on it, on the other side, and there was no one at all in the coach. It was quite, quite empty."

" Did you not think it was Dr. Blewett come to see you, my little man ? "

" No, papa, I did not think anything about whose coach it was. But when it remained at the door, and no one got out, I saw it must be staying for some one to enter it."

"And did any one come out of the house?"

Then the little boy began to sob again, and cling round his father's neck, and kiss him.

" Well, my dear Giles ? "

" Oh, papa !—you will not go away!—I saw you come out of the door, and you went away in the coach—"

" I ! " Lord Lamerton drew a sigh of relief. The dream of the dear little fellow, associated with his illness, had produced an uneasy effect on his father's mind—he feared it might portend the loss of the boy, but if the carriage waited only for himself—!

" That, papa, was why I cried, and was

frightened. You will not go! you must not go!" The child trembled, clasping his father, and rubbing his wet cheek against his father's face.

Then Lord Lamerton called the nurse from the next room. "Master Giles," he said, "is not thoroughly roused. The current of his thoughts must be diverted. Throw that thick shawl over him. I will carry him down into the drawing-room to my lady, and show him a picture-book. Then he will forget his dream and go to sleep. Come for him in a quarter of an hour."

The nurse did as required. Then Lord Lamerton stood up, carrying his son, who laid his head on his father's shoulders, and so he bore him through the passages and down the grand staircase to the drawing-room. The little fair face rested on the shoulder, with the fair hair hanging down over the father's back, and one hand was clutched in the collar. Lord Lamerton kissed the little hand. He was not afraid of making the child's cold worse, the evening was so warm.

Lady Lamerton was sitting on a settee with

a reading lamp on a table at her side, engaged
on an article in one of the contemporary
magazines, on Decay of Belief in the World.

Lady Lamerton was a good woman, who
on Sunday would on no account read a novel,
or a book of travels, or of profane history.
Her Sabbatarianism was a habit that had survived from her childish education, long after
she had come to doubt its obligation or advis-
ability. But, though she would not read a
book of travels, memoirs or history, she had
no scruple in reading religious polemical
literature. On one Sunday she found that
miracles were incredible by intelligent beings,
and next Sunday she had her faith in the
miraculous re-established on the massive
basis of a magazine article.

For an entire fortnight she laboured under
the impression that Christianity had not a
leg to stand on, and then, on the strength of
another article, was sure it stood on as many
as a centipede. For a while she supposed
that dogmas were the cast cocoons of a living
religion, and then, newly instructed, harboured
the belief that it was as impossible to pre-

N

serve the spirit of religion without them as it
is to keep essences without bottles. At one
time she supposed the articles of the creed to
be the shackles of faith, and then that they
were the characters by which faith was de-
cipherable.

The sun was at one time supposed to be a
solid incandescent ball, but astronomers
probed it with their proboscises, and found
that the body was enveloped in sundry wraps,
which they termed photosphere and chromosphere, and which acted as jacket and overcoat to the body, which was declared to be
black as that of a Hottentot. Some fresh
proboscis-poking revealed the fact that the
blackness supposed to be the sun-core was in
fact an intervening vapour or rain of ash, and
when this was perforated, the very body of
the sun was seen, red as that of an Indian,
sullenly glowing, lifeless, almost lightless, a
cinder. Moreover, the spectroscope was
brought to analyse the constituents of the
photosphere and to determine the metals in a
state of incandescence composing it.

Lady Lamerton, looking through the

telescopes of magazine articles and reviews, was continually seeing deeper into the great luminous, heat-giving orb of Christianity; was shown behind its photosphere, taught to despise its chromosphere, and saw exhibited behind them blackness, exhausted force, the ash of extinct superstitions. The critical spectroscope was, moreover, brought to bear on Christianity, and to analyse its luminous atmosphere, and resolve it into alien matter, none distinctively solar, all vulgar, terrestrial, and fusible.

The astronomer assures us that the fuel of the sun must fail, and then the world will congeal and life disappear out of it, and the critic announces the speedy expiring of Christianity. But, as—indifferent to the fact that the sun like a worn-out and made-up old beau is tottering to extinction—Lady Lamerton ordered summer bonnets, and laid out new azalea beds, just so was it with her religion. She continued to teach in Sunday-school, went to church regularly, read the Bible to sick people, did her duty in society, ordered her household, made home very dear to his lordship—in a word, lived in the light and heat of that same Christianity which she was assured, and by fits and starts believed, was an exploded superstition. As Lord Lamerton brought little Giles in his arms into the drawing-room, he whispered in his ear, " Not a word about the coach to mamma," and Giles nodded.

Lady Lamerton put her book aside and looked up.

" Oh, Lamerton ! What are you doing ? The boy is unwell, and ought to be in bed."

" He has been dreaming, my dear ; has had the nightmare, and I have brought him down for change, to drive the frightening thoughts away. He will not take cold, he is in flannel, and the shawl is round him. Besides, the evening is warm."

" He must not be here many minutes. He ought to be asleep," said his mother.

" My dear, I have promised him a look at a picture-book. It will make him forget his fancies. What have you over there ? "

" No Sunday stories or pictures, I fear."

"Yonder is a book in red—illustrated. What is it?"

"'Sintram'—it is not a Sunday book."

"I have not read it for an age, but if I remember right, the D— comes into it."

"If that be the case it is perhaps al ow-able."

"What is the meaning of that picture?" asked the little boy, pointing to the first in the text. It was by Selous. It represented a great hall with a stone table in the centre, about which knights were seated, carousing. In the foreground was a boy kneeling, beat-ing his head, apparently frantic. An old priest stood by, on one side, and a baron was starting from the table, and upsetting his goblet of wine.

"I cannot tell, I forget the story, it must be forty years since I read it. I have not my glasses. Pass the book to your mother, she will read."

Lady Lamerton drew the volume to her, and read as follows :—"A boy, pale as death, with disordered hair and closed eyes, rushed into the hall, uttering a wild scream of terror, and clinging to the baron with both hands, shrieked piercingly, 'Knight and father! Father and knight! Death and another are closely pursuing me!' An awful stillness lay like ice on the whole assembly, save that the boy screamed ever the fearful words."

"It is not a pretty story," said Lord Lamerton uneasily.

"Papa," whispered the boy, "I did not think that anything was following me. I thought"—his father's hand pressed his shoulders—"no, papa, I will not repeat it to mamma."

"What is it, Giles?" asked his mother, looking up from the book.

"Nothing but this, my dear," answered Lord Lamerton, "that I told Giles not to talk about his dreams. He must forget them as quickly as possible."

"What is that priest doing?" asked the child, pointing to the picture.

Lady Lamerton read further. "'Dear Lord Biorn,' said the chaplain, 'our eyes and thoughts have all been directed to you and your son in a wonderful manner; but so it has been ordered by the providence of God.'"

"I think, Giles, we will have no more of 'Sintram' to-night. Let us look together at the album of photographs. I will show you the new likeness of Aunt Hermione."

"Where is young Mr. Saltren?" asked Lady Lamerton.

"I fancy he has gone to see his mother. If I remember aright, he said, after dinner, that he would stroll down to Chillacot."

"There comes nurse," said Lady Lamerton. "Now, Giles, dear, you must go to sleep, and sleep like a top."

"I will try, dear mamma." But he clung to and kissed most lovingly, and still with a little distress in his flushed face, his father. He had not quite shaken off the impression left by his dream. When the boy was going out at the door, keeping his head over his nurse's shoulder, wrapped in the shawl, Lord Lamerton watched him lovingly. Then ensued a silence of a minute or two. It was broken by Lady Lamerton who said—

"We really cannot go on any longer in the crypt."

" The crypt ? "

" You must build us a new school-room. The basement of the keeper's cottage is un· endurable. It did as a make-shift through the winter, but in summer the closeness is insupportable. Besides, the noises overhead preclude teaching and prevent learning."

" I will do what I can," said Lord Lamerton ; "but I want to avoid building this year, as I am not flush of money. Such a room will cost at least four hundred pounds. It must have some architectural character, as it will be near the church, and must not be an eyesore. I wish it were possible to set the miners to build, so as to relieve them ; but they are incapable of doing anything outside their trade."

" What will they do ? "

" I cannot say. They have not been like the young larks in the fable. These were alarmed when they overheard the farmer and his sons discuss the cutting of the corn. But the men have been forewarned and have taken no notice of the warnings. Now they are bewildered and alarmed because they are turned off."

" Something must be done for them."

" I have been considering the cutting of a new road to the proposed station ; but the position of the station cannot be determined till Saltren has consented to sell Chillacot, and he is obstinate and stupid about it."

" Then you cannot cut it till you know where the station will be ? "

" Exactly ; and Captain Saltren is obstructive.   I am not at all sure that his right to the land could be maintained.   I strongly suspect that I might reclaim it ; but I do not wish any unpleasantness."

" Of course not.   Is the road necessary ? "

" Not exactly necessary ; but I suppose work for the winter must be found for the men.   As we have not gone to town this season, and if, as I propose, we abandon our projected tour to the Italian lakes in the autumn, I daresay we can manage both the road and the school-room ; but I need not tell you, Julia, that I have had heavy losses.

My Irish property brings me in not a groat.
I have lost heavily through the failure of the
Occidental Bank, and I have reduced my
rents. I am sorry for the men. Cornish
mining is bad, or the fellows might have gone
to Cornwall. Perhaps if I find them work
on the new road, mines may look up next
year."

"Arminell has been speaking to me about
Samuel Ceely. She wants him taken on,"
said her ladyship. "She will pay for him
out of her own pocket."

Lord Lamerton's mouth twitched. "Arminell has asked me why I should have been
allowed two Lady Lamertons, and he not
one Mrs. Ceely."

"Arminell is an odd girl," said her lady
ship. "But I am thankful to find her take
some interest in the poor. It is a new phase
in her life."

"It seems to me," said Lord Lamerton,
" that you and Armie are alike in one
particular, and unlike in another. You both
puzzle your brains with questions beyond
your calibre, you with theological, she with

social questions ; but you are unlike in this, that you take your perplexities easily, Arminell goes into a fever over hers."

" It is a bitter sorrow to me that I cannot influence her," said Lady Lamerton humbly. " But I believe that no one devoid of definite opinions could acquire power over her. I see that so much can be said, and said with justice on all sides of every question, that all my opinions remain, and ever will remain, in abeyance."

" I sincerely trust that the minx will not fall under the influence of those who are opinionated."

" Arminell is young, vehement, and, as is usual with the young, indisposed to make allowance for those who oppose what commends itself to her mind, or for those who do not leap at conclusions with the same activity as herself."

" And she is pert ! " said Lord Lamerton. " Upon my soul, Julia, it is going a little too far to take me to task for having been twice married. And again, when I said something about my being content with the providential ordering of the world, she caught me up, and told me that anyone with a coronet and fifty thousand a year would say the same. I have not that sum this year, anyhow. Girls nowadays are born without the bump of reverence, and with that of self-assurance unduly developed."

Neither spoke for a few minutes.

Presently Lord Lamerton, who was looking depressed, and was listening, said :

" Hark ! Is that Giles crying again ? "

" I heard nothing."

" Possibly it was but my fancy. Poor little fellow ! Something has upset him. It was unfortunate, Julia, our lighting on ' Sintram.'"

He stood up.

" I am not easy about the dear little creature. Did you see, Julia, how he kissed me, and clung to me ? "

" He is very fond of you, Lamerton."

" And I of him. I think I shall be more easy if I go up and see our Sintram, and learn whether he is asleep, or whether the bad dreams are threatening him. Poor little Sintram ! "

" You will come back, Lamerton ? "

" Yes, dear, when I have seen and kissed my little Sintram."

CHAPTER XIII.

THE PRIVILEGED CLASS.

" Is it not a sad reflection," said Lady Lamerton on the return of his lordship, "that the men who influence others are those of one idea, in a word, the narrow ? Because they are *borné* in mental vision, ignorant and prejudiced, they throw the whole force of their wills in one direction, they become battering rams, and the harder their heads the heavier the blows they deal. If we have knowledge, breadth of vision, charity, we cease to be certain, are no longer bigots, and our power of impressing others fails in proportion to our liberality. I feel my own incompetence with Arminell, but not with Arminell alone. I am conscious of it when taking my Sunday class. I dare insist on nothing, because I am convinced of nothing. I am so much afraid of laying stress on any religious topic, which has been, is, or may be controverted, that I restrain myself to the explanation of those facts which I know to be indisputable. I teach the children that when Ahasuerus sent young men with letters riding on dromedaries, these animals had two humps; whereas when Rebekah lighted down off her camel to meet Isaac, her creature had but one hump. And I console the dying with the last bulletins of the Palestine Exploration Fund determining the site of Ezion Geber. You know, my dear Lamerton, that there are in the atmosphere nitrogen which is the negative gas, oxygen which is positive, and carbonic acid which is deleterious to life. I suppose it is the same with the spiritual atmosphere breathed by the soul, only the oxygen is so hard—nay, to me so impossible to extract, and I am so scrupulous not to communicate any carbonic acid to my scholars, that I fill the lungs of their souls with nitrogen only—a long category of negatives."

"What you teach matters little. The great fact of your kindness and sympathy and sense of duty remains undisturbed, unassailable," said Lord Lamerton.

" My dear," said her ladyship, " I wish I
could be of more use than I am ; but I am
like Mrs. Quickly in the ' Merry Wives of
Windsor,' who held commissions simul-
taneously for Doctor Caius, Slender and
Fenton, and wished each and all success in
his suit for sweet Anne Page. I am not a
power, or anything appreciable, because my
judgment hangs ever in suspense and flickers
like a needle in a magnetic storm. When I
hear our dear good rector lay down the law
with thump of cushion in the pulpit, I know
he is thoroughly sincere and that sincerity is
the outcome of conviction. All this emphasis
would go were he to read such-or-such an
article in the *Westminster Review*, because
his conviction would be sapped. But, without his conviction would he be of much use ?
Would he carry weight with his rustic au-
dience? They value his discourses as the
Israelite valued the strong blast that brought
quails. If his mighty lungs blew nothing but
vagueness, would they care to listen, or if
they listened would they pick up anything
where nothing was dropped ? I am sure that

the great leaders of men were men of one
idea. Look at the apostles, illiterate fisher-
men, but convinced, and they upset heathen-
dom. Look at Mahomet, an epileptic mad-
man, believing absolutely in only one thing—
himself, and he founded Islam. Calvin, Luther,
St. Bernard, Hildebrand, all were men of one
idea, allowing of no *Ifs* and *Buts* to qualify.
That was the secret of their strength. It is
the convex glass that kindles a fire, not that
which is even."

"The narrow can only influence the
ignorant."

"The narrow will always influence the
bulk of men, for the bulk of mankind is
ignorant, not perhaps of the three R's, but of
the compensating forces which keep the
social and political systems from flying to
pieces."

"Thank heaven, Julia, the country is not
in the hands of fanatics to whirl her to
destruction."

"How long will it remain so? There are
plenty of hot-brained Phaethons who think
themselves capable of driving the horses of

the sun, and who have not yet learned to
control themselves. To my mind, Lamerton, our class is the fly-wheel that saves the
watch from running down at a gallop, and
marking no progress at all. In the chron-
ometer the balance-wheel is made up of two
metals with different powers of contraction
and expansion, one holds the other in check,
and produces equilibrium. The wheel os-
cillates this way, that way, and acts as a con-
trolling power on the mainspring, and modi-
fies the action of the wheels. Our class is so
constituted with its double character, is so
brought into relation with all parties in
politics, is so associated with every kind of
interest in the country, that it is swung this
way, that way, is kept in perpetual vibration,
and acts as an effective regulator on the
violent forces in the political and social
world—forces confined, and strong because
confined, forces which keep the machine
going, but which uncontrolled would wreck
it."

"I dare say you are right, Julia. I have
no doubt the social classes are all as, and

where they ought to be, superposed as geologic strata, but wonderfully contorted, it must be allowed, in places. To change the subject—what have you said to Arminell about that fellow for whom she pleaded?"

"Samuel Ceely?"

"Yes, that is his name."

"He is a poor creature," said Lady Lamerton, "a cripple."

"If I remember right he was a scamp at one time and got into one or two scrapes, but what they were, 'pon my soul I do not remember."

"He is harmless enough now," said Lady Lamerton. "I have him on my list of those for whom I pay into the shoe-club, and the clothing-club, the blanket and the coal clubs. The rector's wife said it was a pity he should miss the advantages, which he must do, as he is too poor to pay, and he needs them more than many who receive them. So I have him on my list of those for whom I pay. I have told Arminell that he can work in the glen. That requires to be done up, it has been neglected for so many years. The paths and summer-house, the benches, the water-fall, are all out of order. Giles may like to play there. Arminell will pay the man out of her allowance, it is her own wish. And now, Lamerton, I also will change the subject, and that to one which I am not sure I ought to mention on a Sunday. I am glad for one thing, that we do not go to town for the season, as it will enable us to show some civility to the country people, the squires and the parsons. Really, when we have the house full of our friends, we cannot do it the groups do not amalgamate, they have so few subjects in common. I have thought of a garden-party for Wednesday week. You will mind and make no engagements for that day."

"I will book it—to be at home on Wednesday week." Lord Lamerton seated himself, and the light of his wife's reading lamp fell on his face.

"Are you not feeling well?" she asked. "You look pale, dear."

"It is nothing," he replied. "I may have

caught a slight chill in the avenue, as no
doubt the dew is falling, and there are no
clouds in the sky. The night is very still
and lovely, Julia. No—I think not—no, I
cannot have been chilled there. I do not
know what it is. Well—I will not say that
either. To tell you the whole truth, I am
worried."

"Worried? About what?"

"I am uneasy, for one thing, about Arminell. She has got queer fancies in her
head. Giles also is not well; and there is
something further—in itself nothing, but
though a trifle it is distressing me greatly."

"What is it?"

"The leaders of my choice pines, which
I had planted about the grounds, have been
maliciously cut off. The thing has been
done out of spite, and to hurt me, and yet
the real sufferers are yet unborn. A hundred years hence these trees would have
been admired for their stateliness—and now
they are mutilated. I shall be dead and
forgotten long before any tree I have put in
comes to size. I am pained—this has been

aimed at me, to wound me. I fear this has been done because I have refused to allow my house to be undermined."

" Who can have done it ? "

" I do not know. If I did know, I would not prosecute. That is one of the privileges of our privileged class—to bear injuries and impertinences without resentment. I am hurt—I am hurt greatly. The matter may be a trifle "—his lordship stood up—" but— after all I have done for the Orleigh people —it does seem unkind."

Lady Lamerton put out her hand, and took that of her husband. " Never mind," she said ; " he who did it will come to regret it."

" The injury does not touch the Lamertons alone," said his lordship ; " we throw open the park and gardens every Saturday to the public, and we allow Bands of Hope, and Girls' Friendly Societies, and Choirs, and all sorts of agglomerations of men to come here and picnic in our grounds and strew them with sandwich papers and empty gingerbeer bottles, and cut their initials on the park gates and trees. A century hence the trees that have been mutilated would have grown into magnificence, and overshadowed heaven knows what—political, social or religious holiday-taking companies and awkward squads."

"Put in some more pines, next autumn."

"What with rabbits and the public, planting is discouraging work. It costs a lot of money, and you get no satisfaction from it. My dear Julia, it is one of the privileges—no —drawbacks of our class, that we expose a wide surface to the envious and the evil-disposed. They can injure us in a thousand ways, whereas our powers of self-protection are unduly limited. If we try to save ourselves, we do ourselves injury, as pigs when swimming cut their own throats with their fore-claws."

"Never mind that. Whom shall we invite,—or rather, whom must we omit? I must send out cards of invitations to our garden party at once."

"O, bother the garden party," said his lordship wearily. "You and I hardly ever get a quiet evening together, so now that we have one, let us forget the world outside and some of these exacting and embarrassing duties we owe it. Really, I envy those who, belonging to a less conspicuous sphere, have their cosy evenings at home, their privacy and peaceful joys. We are forced to live in publicity, we have to fill our house with guests, lay ourselves out to entertain them, keep a French cook for them—I am sure boiled mutton and caper sauce would content me,— stock our cellars for them, keep hunters and preserve the game for them. Upon my word, Julia, we are not suffered to live for ourselves. A selfish existence is with us im possible. No monks or nuns ever gave up half so much, and lived so completely for others, continually sacrificing their own pleasures, leisure, thoughts, time, to others,— as we, the British aristocracy."

"You are out of spirits to-night, Lamerton." His wife retained his hand, and pressed it.

" Then," continued his lordship, following his own train of thought, and not answering his wife's remark, perhaps because he did not hear it, so full was his mind of the topic then

uppermost in it, " then, Julia, consider—we
are mounted specimens ; like those unfortunate worms in sour paste, and monsters
in a drop of dirty water, we were shown by
lime-light and a magnifying glass the other
evening at the National School, projected
on a white sheet. The whole room was
crowded, and the bumpkins in the place sat
gazing as the lecturer pointed to the wriggling
creatures, named each in succession, and
described it. What must have been the discomfort to those animals, if in any degree
sensitive, to be exposed, stared at, glared
through, commented on ! and—consider—
the lecturer may have misinterpreted them,
because misunderstanding them, and they
listened to it all, squirmed a little more pain-
fully, but were incapable of setting him to
rights. The German princes are entitled
durch-laucht, that is, ' Transparencies ; ' and
quite right. We also are transparencies, we
worms of the aristocracy, monsters of
privilege, held up before the public eye,
magnified, projected on newspaper sheets,
characterised sometimes aright, more often

wrongly, forced to have every nerve in our
system, every pulsation in our blood, every
motion in our brains, every moment in our
lives, and every writhe of our bodies and
spasm of our hearts commented on by the
vulgar, and brutally misunderstood. It is
rather hard on us, Julia. There are other
worms in the sour paste of life, other
monsters in the drop of dirty water we call
Society, who are at liberty to turn about, and
stretch themselves, bound or coil as they list;
only we—we must live and wriggle between
two plates of glass, illuminated and made
translucent by the most powerful known light,
denied that privilege which belongs to the
humble—opacity."

"Is it the injured pines that have put you
out of spirits to-night, Lamerton?" asked my
lady, stroking the hand she held.

" Did you ever read about Matthew
Hopkins, the witch finder?" asked his lordship, with a fluttering smile on his lips.
" He brought many poor harmless creatures
to a violent end. Every suspected witch
was stripped and closely examined for a mole,

a wart, for any blemish,—and such blemishes
were at once declared to be the devil's seals,
stamping the poor wretches as his own.
Then they were tied hand and foot together,
and thrown into the water ; if they sank they
were pronounced innocent ; if they floated
they were declared guilty and were withdrawn from the water to be delivered over to
fire.   We, Julia, are treated in a way not unlike that pursued by Matthew Hopkins ; and
there are ten thousand amateur witch-finders
searching us, tearing off our clothes, peering
after defects, chucking us into the water or the
fire.   If we are found to have moles, how we
are probed with lancets, and plucked with
tweezers, and then we are cast to the flames
of public indignation and democratic wrath.
If, however, we are found to have no moles
about us, if we give no occasion for scandal,
then away we are pitched into water, and
down down we sink in public estimation, and
chill disregard, as coroneted nonentities."

Lady Lamerton continued to caress her
husband's hand.

"Then again," he continued, after a short

silence, " the witches were tortured into confession by sleeplessness. They were seated
on uncomfortable stools, and watched night
and day. If they nodded, their soles were
tickled with feathers, cold water was poured
down their backs, or pepper was blown up
their noses. As for us, it is the same, we are
not allowed to live quietly, we are forced to
activity. I am kept running about, giving
prizes at school commemorations, taking seat
on committees, laying foundation-stones,
opening institutions, attending quarter sessions, throwing wide my doors to every one,
my purse to a good many ; I am denied
domesticity, denied rest. I am kept in perpetual motion. I have a title, that means
every one else has a title to bully me. I am
tickled into energy if I nod, or the pepper of
journalistic sarcasm is blown into my eyes
and nose to stir me to activity. Julia, a rich
merchant, or banker, or manufacturer, a well-
to-do tradesman lives more comfortably than
do we. In the first place, they can do what
they will with their money—but we have to
meet a thousand claims on what we get, and

are grudged the remnant we reserve for our
individual enjoyment, Next, they are not
exposed to ruthless criticism, to daily, hourly
comment, as are we. They are free, we are
not ; they can think first of themselves, afterwards of others, whereas we have to be for
ever considering others, and thrusting ourselves into corners, thankful to find a corner
in which we may possess and stretch our individual selves. Upon my soul, I wish I had
been born in another order of humanity, without title, and land, and a seat in the Upper
House, and—and without manganese."

" If it had been so—"

" If it had been so, then I could have en-
joyed life, stuck at home, and seen more of you,
and Arminell, and dear little Giles, and then
—why then, I would have had no enemies."

Lord Lamerton had reseated himself when
he began to talk of Matthew Hopkins, the
witch-finder. Now he stood up again.

" Julia," he said, " those Douglas pines had
made noble shoots—it is a pity. I shall go
to bed, and dream, if I can, that I am lying
in clover and not over a bunch of manganese."

CHAPTER XIV.

MR. JAMES WELSH.

MRS. SALTREN had informed Arminell that she had a brother who was a gentleman. The term "gentleman" is derived from the Latin *gens*, and signifies a member of a patrician family. But this is not the signification now given it in the vernacular. On the tongue of the people, a gentleman and a lady are those who do no manual labour. A man informs you that he will be a gentleman on a bank-holiday, because he will lounge about with his hands in his pockets, and an old woman who has weeded turnips at ninepence a day becomes a lady when rheumatism invades her limbs, and sends her to the union.

Mr. James Welsh, the brother of Mrs. Saltren, was a gentleman in this, that he belonged to a *gens*, a class not ancient or aristocratic, but modern, and one that has obtained considerable influence, wields much power and is likely to become dominant—we mean that of the professional journalist and politician. He was a gentleman also in this, that he did no hard manual labour, but few men worked harder than he, but then he dirtied his hands with ink only.

Along the coasts of Scotland and Sweden are terraces raised high above the sea-level, which are pronounced by geologists to be ancient beaches. At one time the waves washed where now sheep graze, and deposited sea-weed and shells where now grow heather and harebells. There are these raised sea-beaches in man, to which conscience at one time reached, where it formed a barrier, and whence it has retreated. But we are wrong in speaking of the retreat of the sea, for actually the level of the ocean is permanent, it is the land which rises, and as it rises leaves the sea below. And so perhaps it is with us. We lift ourselves above old convictions, scruples, principles, and the sometimes sleeping, sometimes tossing sea of conscience no longer touches those points they once fretted. Do we congratulate ourselves on this elevation? Perhaps so, and yet few of us can contemplate the raised beaches left in our hearts by the retiring waves of conscience without a sigh, and a doubt.

Mr. James Welsh said and wrote and did many things as a public journalist and a professional politician which as a boy or young man he would have looked upon as dishonest, false, and mischievous. His conscience no longer troubled him in his business, but in home relations he was blameless.

Perhaps one reason why the sea-level alters with us, is that we are always endeavouring to reclaim land from it, thrusting our sea-walls of self-interest further out, to take in more field from being overwashed. We make our line of conscience co-terminous with our line of self-interest. Outside this line the waves may toss and roar, within they may not cast a flake of foam, or waft a breath of ozone. How much thunder and buffet we permit outside our sea-wall of self-interest against any rock or sand-bank that stands unenclosed! but we only suffer the water of self-reproach to sweep with a shallow swash and soothing murmur the outside of the bank we have cast up.

What excellent words those are to conjure with and wherewith blind our own eyes as well as those of others—Political Party and The Public Weal! We regard ourselves as devoted to the *respublica*, when, in reality, we care only for our private interests; and our zeal for the public good is hot or cold according as our dividends are affected.

If we can show that the welfare of our party can be advanced by making out our neighbour to be a thief and assassin, with what pious energy do we set to work to invent lies to defame him. How we suppress and disguise facts which make against our pet doctrines! To what subterfuges and tricks do we have recourse to colour those facts which cannot be suppressed, to make them look the opposite to what we know them to be!

It is really deserving of note how every dirty and dishonourable act is wrapped about with a moral sanction, as a comfit with a motto in a cracker.

We always profess to be actuated by noble and disinterested motives, and yet they are generally mean and personal. Our ancestors regarded the planets only so far as they by their conjunctions and interferences with each other's houses affected the constitutions and careers of these ancestors of ours. Jupiter is 1250 times larger than the earth, and has seven moons, and this planet with its moons revolves and illumines the sky to affect the spleen of Master Jack Sparrow and disturb the courtship of Mistress Jenny Wren. Jupiter is distant five-hundred millions of miles from Jack and Jenny—but what of that? According to Euclid a straight line can be drawn between any two given points, accordingly between the planet at one end and these little nobodies at the other, lines exist. Now all people actually do draw invisible lines between themselves and every other object in heaven and earth, and contemplate these objects along these lines, and value and despise them according as these objects affect them along these lines.

The author was travelling in a second-

P

class railway-carriage on that memorable
Monday morning after the Phœnix-Park
tragedy that thrilled all England with horror
and rage. Facing him, sat a gentleman
reading his paper, who ever and anon slapped
his knee, and exclaimed, " Famous ! Splendid ! Nothing better could have happened ! "
Presently, unable to understand these ex-
clamations, the author asked, " Sir ! do you
mean to say that you approve of the crime ? "

"Oh, no ! " was his answer. " Certainly
not, but, consider how it will make the
papers sell ! I have shares in one or two."

The writer was talking the other day to a
timber merchant on the condition of Ireland.
" I trust," said he, " that the Plan of
Campaign will not be suppressed as yet.
We can buy Irish oak at fourpence a foot
just now."

The writer was discussing the annexation
of Alsace with a native farmer. " Well,"
said he, " when we belonged to France I
sold for a franc what I now sell for a
mark, *therefore*, God save Kaiser Wilhelm."
" But," was objected, " probably you now

have to pay a mark for what formerly cost you a franc." He considered for a moment. and then said, " That is true, vive la France ! " Twopence turned his patriotism this way to Berlin, or that way to Paris. He was a German when selling, a Frenchman when buying, all for twopence.

The professional politician is a man who lives by politics as the professional chess-player lives by chess. He acquires a professional conscience. His profession has to fill his pockets and find bread for his children, and politics must be kept going to do so. The chess-player sacrifices pawns to gain his end. The stoker shovels on coals into the furnace to make his engine gallop ; and the electrician pours vitriol into the battery to produce a current in his wires. They have none of them the slightest scruple in doing these things—they belong to the business, and the professional politician has no scruple in playing with facts, and throwing them away as pawns in his game, or of exciting the passions and prejudices of men, or of using the most biting and corroding acid in his endeavours to evoke a current of feeling. When an organist desires to produce a noise, he pulls out stop diapason, and dances on the pedals. The professional politician deals with the public in the same way ; that is his instrument. What in the organ are the pedals for but to be kicked, and the keys but to be struck, and the stops but to be drawn out, and what are the social classes but the manuals, and the individuals composing them, but the keys, and the grudges, greed, ambition, envy, and prejudices but the stops, which a clever player understands to man-ipulate ?

Mr. Welsh was a worthy man, eminently respectable, a good husband, and a kind friend. He was truthful, honest, reliable in his family and social relations, but profes-sionally unscrupulous. The sea-line stood in its old place on one side of his character, but on another a wide tract, that tract on which he grew his harvest, had been re-claimed from the waves of conscience. It is so with a good many others besides Mr. Welsh, and in a good many other trades and professions than journalism and politics. We are conscientious in every department except that of money-making, and in that we allow of tricks and meannesses, which we excuse to ourselves as forced on us by the exigencies of competition. Recently Mr. Welsh had been slightly indisposed, so he came from town into the country, on a holiday, to spend the Sunday with his sister, and then run on to see a congenial friend in a town in the same county.

In the afternoon he took a stroll by himself in the woods, smoking his pipe, and, always with an eye to business, looking about him for material for an article.

" Halloo ! " said Mr. Welsh, halting in front of the ruinous cottage of Patience Kite. " What have we here ? Does any one inhabit this tumble-down concern ? "

He went to the door and looked in.

Patience faced him.

" What do you want ? Who are you ? This is my house, and I will not be turned out of it."

She took him for a sanitary officer, or a lawyer, come to enforce her expulsion.

" This is a queer hole for a lady to occupy as her boudoir," said Mr. Welsh, taking his pipe out of his mouth. " I wouldn't care for this style of thing myself except as a drawing copy. Not to become a hero of romance, or to give my experience in a magazine article would I sleep under that chimney on a stormy night."

" Nobody has invited you," said Patience, blocking her door.

" And pray, madam, whose house is this ? Is this the sort of cottage my lord provides for his tenants ? "

" The house is mine."

" Copyhold or freehold ? "

" I pay a ground rent for it of two shillings ; it is mine for life, and then it falls to his lordship."

" I should expect it would fall altogether to you shortly. Why don't you do it up ? "

' How can I ? I am poor."

" I suppose that you are bound by the terms of the lease to maintain the house in repair ? "

" I dare say. The agent, Mr. Macduff,

has threatened me ; but no one can make me do it when I haven't a shilling. You can't make one dance who is born without legs."

" Then, properly this house belongs to his lordship. Why does not he do it up ? I can make something out of this ! A Day in the Country, something to fill a column and a-half in a Monday morning paper. Contrast his lordship's princely residence with the ruins in which he pigs his tenants. Compare Saltren's place, Chillacot, which is his own, all in spic-and-span order, with this, and then a word about the incubus of the great holders on the land, and the advantage of the enfranchisement of the soil. It will do. And so, madam, they have tried to evict you ? "

"Yes ; the sanitary officer ordered me to leave, the Board of Guardians went to the magistrates, and issued a summons to me to quit, and my lord has sent Mr. Macduff to me, to threaten proceedings against me if I will not put the house in repair or quit it. But what can they do when I won't budge, and could prosecute 'em if they laid fingers on me? The police daren't touch me. They've come and looked at me and argued, but they can't force me to leave."

" So his lordship wants to evict you, eh ? "

" Mr. Macduff has declared he'll send masons and strip the roof, and pull down the chimney, and rebuild the walls, but they can't do it without driving me out first, and that is more than they can with me having the house as my own for life."

" By Jove ! " exclaimed Welsh, "it's a case—a poor widow, I suppose you are a widow ; it doesn't matter if you are not ; it sounds best—a widow, a victim to his lordship's tyranny—tearing down the roof that shelters her grey head, casting down her chimney, desecrating her hearthstone, the sacred penates, with the foot of violence—or hoof, which shall it be ? By George ! I'll make something out of it, harrowing to the feelings, and as rousing as tartaric acid and soda ! Who cares for a contradiction or a correction ? We can always break the lines and make nonsense of it, and lay the blame on the printer, if called to task. I'm glad I came here for a Sunday. You will let me inside, I suppose, ma'am, to cast an eye round ; particulars are so useful in a description, lend such a *vraisemblance* to an account."

But Mrs. Kite's tumble-down cottage was not the only material Mr. Welsh collected for use on that Sunday. He heard from Saltren about the stoppage of the manganese.

"Something can be made out of that," said Welsh. "We are in want of a grievance. Tell me the particulars, I'll sift out for myself what will serve my purpose."

When he had heard all, "It will do," said he, "there has been nothing to interest the public or stir them up since the last divorce suit in high life. High life !—so high that some folks had to hold their noses. We want a bit of a change now. After that bit of strong venison, some capsicum to restore the palate. Saltren, you must convene a public meeting, make a demonstration, a torchlight procession of the out-of-work, issue a remonstrance. I'll come and help you. I know how to work those kind of things.

A little grievance and some dissatisfaction well-stirred together is like chlorate of potash and sulphur in a mortar, only stir away, and in the end you get an explosion."

" It is of no use," said the captain, in a tone of discouragement.

" Of no use ! I tell you it is of the utmost use ; we'll make a public matter of it. Get a question asked in the House about it. There are so many journalists in there now that we can get anything asked when we want the question as a text for a leader. Why, we will fill the papers with your grievance, only we must have some meeting to report, and I'll help you with that. Bless you, I've half a dozen ways of poking this matter into notoriety ; and we will show up the British aristocracy as the oppressors of the poor, those who are driving business out of the country, who are the true cause of the prevailing depression. Thanks to that recent divorce case we've made them out to be the moral cancer in the body of old England, and now we shall show that they are the drag on commercial progress. When folks are grumbling because the times are bad, it makes them mighty content to be shown a cause for it all, on which they may vent their ill-humour. Did you ever read ' The Curiosity Shop,' Saltren ? Quilp had a figure-head to batter whenever things went wrong with him, and the public are much like Quilp ; give 'em an admiral or a peer, or an archbishop, some figure-head, and whack, bang, hammer, and smash they go at it."

" As for the aristocracy," said Mrs. Saltren, " I ought to know them. I combed their hair, and hooked their dresses, and un-packed their portmanteaus ; and them as do that are best qualified to know them, I should think."

" I don't mind telling you," said the captain, addressing his brother-in-law, " that their doom is sealed in heaven. I've had it re-vealed to me."

" You have, have you ? " asked Welsh in a tone of irony, which, however, Saltren did not perceive.

" Yes, I have—you shall hear. I would not tell every one, but I tell you. I was in the spirit this very morning, and I heard a voice from heaven, saying unto me, Saltren, Saltren! Then I looked, and behold there came flying down to me, a book from heaven, written within and without. I held up my hands to receive it; but it fell past me into the water, and I stooped and looked thereon, and saw written ' The Gilded Clique,' and again the voice cried, ' It is fallen, it is fallen!'"

" You don't expect me to gulp that——" Welsh checked himself, and added, shaking his head —" I can't, I'm afraid, make copy of that."

" It is true," said Saltren earnestly. His vehemence, his kindled eyes, his deepened colour, showed his sincerity. " Would I dare in such matters to utter lies? I am but a poor mean instrument, but what of that? Prophets have been found among shepherds, and apostles taken from their fishing nets. I was engaged in heartfelt prayer when this took place."

" You didn't happen to fall asleep, whilst occupied in devotion, of course?" said Welsh, with a contemptuous jerk of the chin. 'Such a weakness is not likely to befall you."

"I was not asleep," answered Saltren sternly. "How could I be asleep, when my eyes were open, and I saw the book ; and my ears, and they heard the voice ? "

"You didn't happen to get hold of the book, and see the name of the publisher ? "

"No—I was unable. It was unnecessary. I read the title plainly. I saw what was on the cover of the book."

"I can do nothing with this," said Welsh, leaning back in his chair, stretching, and closing his hands behind the back of his head.

This belongs to another department altogether. You had better relate your experiences at the next revival-meeting among the horse-marines, there is no knowing what effect it may have upon that intelligent and excitable body of men."

"It is true," urged Saltren again, frowning.

He was incapable of seeing that his brother-in-law was bantering him. The man was absolutely without sense of humour ; but he saw that Welsh did not believe in his story,

and this irritated and offended him.   That his
tale, as he told it, grew in its proportions and
became more and more unreal, was also what
he did not know.   His mind worked on the
small materials it had, and spun out of them
a fable in which he himself implicitly believed.

"I don't dispute what you have narrated,"
said Welsh composedly.   "I know you are a
total abstainer, so it is not to be accounted
for in the way which comes naturally uppermost.   Still, I've heard of wonderful elevation
of spirits and general head-over-heeledness
after an over-dose of non-alcoholic efferves-
cing liquors."

"I had touched nothing," said Saltren,
with his temper chafed.   "If you doubt
me——"

"But I do not doubt you," interrupted
Welsh.   "I tell you that this does not
interest me, because it is outside my department, like Bulgaria, and the Opera Comique,
and Inoculations for Hydrophobia, and
Primitive Marriage.   I don't meddle with
the Eastern Question, or review historical
works, or sermons, or novels.   I leave all

that to other fellows; you must pass this on to the chap who does religion, not that I think he would make copy out of it for a magazine article, except under the head of Hallucinations."

CHAPTER XV.

" Now look straight for'ard," said Mr. Welsh, "and distinguish. You call this affair of yours and the book—a revelation. There are revelations, my friend, that may be written with a capital R, and others that have to begin with a small cap."

Mr. Welsh was not particular about the English he spoke, but he wrote it well, at least passably.

" The sort of revelation that suits me, one with a capital R, is that at which a shorthand reporter assists. That's the sort of revelation we get in the courts—that is, as the French say, *controlé*. But on the other hand comes your hole-and-corner revelation, which has more given it than is its due when written with a little *r*. No reporter, no public present, totally uncontrolled ; that sort of revelation is no use to me. I don't mean to say but that sort of thing may go down at revivals, but for the press it is no good at all."

"Am I likely to have imagined it? What should have put the thought of ' The Gilded Clique ' into my head ? " asked Saltren angrily. " I tell you I believe in this revelation as I believe that I see you before me."

" Gilded Clique ! " repeated Welsh, " I can't say, but Gaboriau's criminal novel may have fallen under your eyes."

" What is that ? "

" A French novel with that title. It has been translated."

" Now see ! " exclaimed Captain Saltren, kindling, springing up, and waving his arms, " I never have set eyes on such a book, never heard of it before. But nothing that you could have said would have confirmed me in my conviction more than this. It shows that the devil is active, and that to draw away attention from, and to weaken the force of my revelation, he has caused a book to be circulated under the same name. I should not be surprised if you told me it had a blood-red cover."

" It has one."

"There!" cried Saltren, "now nothing
will ever shake my faith. When the devil
strives to defeat the purposes of Heaven, it
is because he fears those purposes. My
solemn and sincere conviction is——" He
lowered his voice, but though low it shook
with emotion. "My belief is that the book
I saw was the Everlasting Gospel. John
saw an angel flying in heaven having that
book in his right hand, but it was not then
communicated to man. The time was not
ripe. Now, at last, towards the end of the
ages, that book has been cast down, and its
purport disclosed."

"You didn't happen to see the angel?"
asked Welsh sneeringly.

"I—I am not sure, I saw something.
Indeed, there no doubt was an angel flying,
but my eyes were blinded with the extraordinary light, and my mind has not yet
sufficiently recovered for me to recollect all
the particulars of the vision. But this I can
tell you, for I know it. Although I did not
get hold of the book, its contents are written

in fire in my brain. That book of the Everlasting Gospel declares that the age of
privilege is at an end, the distinctions between
rich and poor; noble and common, are at an
end. This has been hidden from the world,
because the world was not ready to receive
it. Now the time is come, and I am the
humble instrument chosen for announcing
these good tidings to men. I care not if,
like Samson, I be crushed as I take hold of
the pillars, and bow myself, and bring the
House of Lords down."

"Well," said Welsh, "if you can work
that line in the chapel, well and good. I
keep to my province, and that is the
manganese. Why, Condy's fluid, I fancy, is
permanganate of potash—I can lug that in
somehow."

"Ah!" said Mrs. Saltren, who was becoming impatient at having been left out of
the conversation, "at the park they thought
a deal about Condy's fluid."

"I can manage it in this way," said her
brother, rubbing his hands. "That disin-
fectant has manganese as a constituent.

His lordship, by stopping the manganese mine, cuts off a source of health, a deodorising and disinfecting stream from entering the homes of sickness, and the haunts of fever. Who can say how many lives may be sacrificed by the stopping of Wheal Julia? I'll bring in Condy's fluid with effect. What else is manganese used for?"

"Bleaching, I believe," said Mrs. Saltren.

"Ah!" said Mr. Welsh, "that can be worked in also, and I'll pull old Isabelle of Castile in by the ears as well. She vowed she would not change her smock till a certain city she was besieging had capitulated, and as that city held out three months, judge the colour of her linen. We are all, I presume, to wear Isabelle shirts—or rather cuffs and collars—and use Isabelle sheets and towels, and eat off Isabelle tablecloths, and the ministers of the Established Church to preach in Isabelle surplices, because, forsooth, the supply of manganese is withheld wherewith to whiten them."

"Well, it does seem wrong," said Mrs. Saltren.

"And then," continued her brother, kindling with professional enthusiasm, "after that divorce case, too, when the noble lords and ladies washed their dirty linen in public. You can figure how it will all work out. Here is my Lord Lamerton knows that the titled aristocracy have so much dirty linen at home, that he is determined to prevent the British public from wearing bleached linen at all, lest they should perceive the difference. There is nothing," continued Welsh with a chuckle, "nothing so convenient for one's purpose as well mixing one's hyperboles and analogies, and drawing just any conclusions you like out of premises well muddled up with similitudes. We know very well, my dear Marianne, that the bread we buy of the bakers is composed of some flour, and some alum, and some plaster-of-paris, and some china-clay, but we don't stop to analyse it at our breakfast ; we cut ourselves a slice, butter it, and pop it into our mouths, and like it a thousand times better than home-made bread made of pure unadulterated flour. It is just the same with political articles and political speeches. There's a lot of stuff of all sorts goes into them besides the flour of pure reason. And the British public don't analyse, they swallow. What they consume they expect to be light and to taste agreeably— they don't care a farthing what it is made up of."

Mr. Welsh took out his pocket-book, and dotted down his ideas. "Of course," said he, talking and laughing to himself, "we must touch this off with a light hand in a semi-jocose, and semi-serious manner. There are some folks who never see a joke, or rather they always see it as something grave. They are like earth-worms—all swallow."

Mr. Welsh put up his knee, interlaced his fingers round it, and began to swing his knee on a level with his chest.

"If you want to rouse the British public," he said, "you must tickle them. You can't do much with their heads, but their feelings are easily roused. Heads!—why there was no getting wisdom out of the head of Jupiter, till it was clove with an axe, and you would not have the skull of the British public more

yielding than that of the king of the gods."
He put down his leg that he had been hug-
ging. " My dear sister," he went on, " I
know the British public, it is my business to
study it and treat it. I know its moods, and
it is one of the most docile of creatures to
drive. There is one thing it loves above
anything, and that is a sore. Do you remember how Aunt Susan had a bad leg, and
how she went on about that leg, the pride
she took in it, the medicines she swallowed
for it, and how she hated Betsy Tucker
because she also had a bad leg, and how she
contended that hers was the worst, the most in-
flamed, and caused her most pain ? It is so
with the public. It must have its sore ; and
show it, and discuss it, and apply to it quack
plasters, and drink for it quack draughts.
What would the doctors do but for the Aunt
Susans and Betsy Tuckers—their fortunes
stand on these old women's legs. So is it
with us—we live by the bad legs of the
nation. The public, in its heart of hearts,
don't want those precious legs to be healed—
certainly not to be taken off. What we have

to do is to keep the sores angry with caustic, and poked with needles. And that is just why I want this manganese now, to rub it into the legs of the public and wake the sores up into irritation once more."

Then Welsh began to whistle between his front teeth and swing his foot again.

" The public," he continued, " are like Job on a dunghill, rubbing its sores. The public has no desire to have the dunghill removed ; it rather likes the warmth. When it nods off into a nap then we stick the prongs of the fork into it, and up it starts excited and angry, and we turn the heap over under its nose, and then it settles down into it again deeper than before."

" I confess I do not know much about the public," said Mrs. Saltren, resolved to have a word ; " but when you come to the aristocracy, why then you are on my ground."

" On your ground," laughed Welsh, " because you were lady's maid at the Park ; that is like the land surveyor claiming a property because he has walked over it with a chain."

"At all events the surveyor knows it," said Mrs. Saltren, with some spirit, "perhaps better than does the owner."

"I admit that you have me there," laughed her brother.

"And," said Mrs. Saltren, "it is pounds on pounds I might have earned by sending information about high life to the society papers; but I was above doing that sort of thing; besides, the society papers were not published at that time. Sometimes there were as many as a dozen or fourteen lady's-maids and as many valets staying in the house with their masters and mistresses, and they were full of the most interesting information and bursting to reveal it, like moist sugar in a paper-bag."

"I'll tell you what it is," said Welsh, "servantdom is becoming a power in the country, just as the press has become. There is no knowing nowadays where to look for the seat of power, it is at the other extremity from the head. In old times the serfs and slaves were not of account at all, and now their direct representatives hold the characters

and happiness of the best in the land in their
hands. The country may have at one time
been directed by its head; it is not so now,
like a fish, it is directed and propelled by its
tail. The servant class at one time was despised, now it is feared; it mounts on its two
wings, the divorce court and the society
press. What opportunities it now has of pay-
ing off old grudges, of pushing itself into
notoriety, of earning a little money. This is
the age of the utilisation of refuse. We find
an employment for what our forefathers, nay,
our fathers cast aside. The rummage of
copper mines is now burnt for arsenic, the
scum of coal-tar makes aniline dyes, and I
hear they are talking of the convertion of
dirty rags by means of vitriol into lump
sugar. It is so in social and political life—
we are using up our refuse, we invest it with
preponderating political influence, we chuck it
into the House of Commons, and right it
should be so; give everything a chance, and
in an age of transformation we must turn up our
social deposits. If it were not so, life would
be a donkey-race with the prize for the last."

" When I was companion to her ladyship," began Mrs Saltren, but was cut short by her brother—

" I beg your pardon, Marianne, when was that ? I only knew you as lady's-maid."

" I was more than that," said Mrs. Saltren flushing.

" Oh, of course, lady without the maid."

" I might, I daresay, have been my lady, and have kept my maid," said Mrs. Saltren, tossing her head, "so there is no point in your sneers, James. You may be a gentleman, but I am a captain's wife, and might have been more."

" Oh, indeed, and how came you not to be more ? "

" Because I did not choose."

" In fact," said Welsh, " you thought you were in for a donkey-race. By George, you have got the prize ! "

" You are really too bad," exclaimed Mrs. Saltren, vexed and angry, " I could tell you things that would surprise you. You think nothing of me because I am not rich or grand, and have to do the house work in my home ;

but I have been much considered in my day,
and admired, and sought. And I have had
my wrongs, which I thought to have carried
with me to my grave, but as you choose to
insult me, your sister, with saying I came in
last at a donkey-race, I will tell you that properly I ought to have come in first."

"And I," said Saltren, standing up, " I insist on your speaking out." He had remained
silent for some time, offended at his brother-
in-law's incredulity, and not particularly interested in what he was saying, which seemed
to him trifling.

" Let us hear," said Welsh, with a curl of
his lips. He had no great respect for his
sister. "You must let me observe in passing that just now you did not come in first
because you wouldn't, and now, apparently, it
is because you weren't allowed."

" I have no wish," said Marianne Welsh,
not noticing the sneer, "to make mischief,
but truth is truth."

"Truth," interposed Welsh, who had the
family infirmity of loving to hear his own
voice, " truth when naked is unpresentable.

The public are squeamish, and turn aside from it as improper; here we step in and frizzle, paint and clothe her, and so introduce her to the public."

"If you interrupt me, how am I to go on?" asked Mrs. Saltren, testily. "I was going to say, when you interrupted with your coarse remarks, that at one time I was a great beauty, and I don't suppose I've quite lost my good looks yet; and I was then very much sought."

"And what is more," said Welsh, "to the best of my remembrance you were not like a slug in a flower-bed, that when sought digs under ground."

"I tell you," continued Mrs. Saltren, with heightened colour, "that I have been sought by some of the noblest in the land."

Welsh looked out of the corners of his eyes at his sister, and said nothing.

"I was cruelly deceived. A great nobleman whom I will not name—"

"Whose title is in abeyance," threw in Welsh.

"Whom I will not name, but might do so if I chose, obtained a licence for a private

marriage, and a minister to perform the cere-
mony, and there were witnesses—the nuptials
took place. Not till several days after did I
discover that I had been basely deceived.
The licence was forged, the minister was a
friend of the bridegroom disguised as a parson, and not in holy orders, and the witnesses
were sworn to secrecy."

"That is your revelation, is it?" asked
James Welsh. "I write it with a small cap.,
and in pica print."

"It is truth."

"The truth, dressed, of course, and not in
tailor-made clothes. I dress the truth myself, but—let me see, never allow of so much
margin for improvers."

Then Welsh stood up.

"I must be off, Marianne, if I am to catch
the train. Saltren, keep the manganese in
agitation, I will be with you and set your
meeting going. Marianne, I can make no
more of your revelation than I can of that
disclosed by your husband. Facts, my dear
sister, in my business are like the wax figures
in Mrs. Jarley's show. They are to be

dressed in the livery of our political colours, and it is wonderful what service they will do thus; but, Marianne, you can't make the livery stand by itself, there must be facts underneath, it matters not of what a wooden and skeleton nature, they hold up the garments. I can't say that I see in what you have told me any supporting facts at all, only a bundle of tumbled, theatrical, romantic rubbish."

CHAPTER XVI.

HOW SALTREN TOOK IT.

MRS. SALTREN, as already said, as Marianne Welsh, had been good-looking and vain, when lady's-maid to the dowager Lady Lamerton, the mother of the present lord. She had never been in the park with Arminell's mother, as she had pretended. She had been lady's-maid only to the dowager, and had left her service precipitately and married Saltren a year before the marriage of my lord. She had been vain, and thought much of; her good looks were gone, her vanity had not departed with them. Her vanity had been wounded by the loss of her husband's esteem. She had harboured anger against him for many years because of his fantastic ideas, and straight-laced morality. No one is perfect, she argued, and Saltren, who pinned his religion on the Bible, ought to have been the first to admit this.

The just man falleth seven times a day, and she had tripped only once in forty-two years— over fifteen thousand days. If she could but raise the veil and look into her husband's past life, argued she, no doubt she would see comical things there. What if she had tripped? Were not the ways of the world slippery? Did she make them slippery? Had she created the world and set it all over with slides? And if a person did slip, was it becoming of such a person to lie whimpering where she had fallen? Did not that show lack of spirit? For her part, after that slight lapse, she had hopped on her feet, shaken her skirts, and warbled a tune.

It is a fact patent to every one, that the further we recede from an object, the smaller it appears. For instance, the dome of St. Paul's when we stand in St. Paul's Churchyard, looks immense. But as we stand on Paul's Wharf, waiting for a steamer, we already discover that the small intervening distance has diminished the dome to the size of a dish-cover. As we descend the river, the cupola decreases in proportion as we

widen our distance from it, till it is reduced to an inconsiderable speck, and finally
sinks beyond the range of our vision. It is
precisely the same with our faults. At the
moment of their commission, from under
their shadow, they look portentous and
actually oppress us ; but they become sensibly
reduced in bulk the farther we drift down
life's stream from them. What immeasur-
ably weighed on us yesterday, measurably
burden us to-day, and to-morrow are per-
ceptible ; but the day after cease to discomfort us. Not so only, but as we draw further
from our past fault, we look back on it with
a sort of fond admiration, tinged with sad-
ness ; we lounge over the bulwarks of our
boat, opera-glass in hand, and consider it as
we consider the dome of St. Paul's, as an
adjunct not altogether regretable in the retro-
spect ; for, consider how uniform, how insufferable would be the landscape, without
breaks in the sky line.

Now Mrs. Saltren was embarked on the
same voyage with Stephen, her husband,
and naturally expected that the same object

which at one moment had obscured their sun,
but which rapidly diminished in size and importance and signification to her eyes, should
equally tend to disappear from his. When,
however, she found that it did not, she was
offended, and harboured the conviction that
she was herself the injured party. Why
were not Stephen's eyes constituted as the
eyes of other men ? She had good occasion
to take umbrage at the perversity of his
vision. She had admitted at one time,
faintly, and with a graceful curtsey, a pretty
apology, and with that reluctance which a
woman has to confess a fault, that her
husband had been an injured man ; but now,
after the lapse of over twenty years, their
relative positions were reversed. The cases
are known of girls who have swallowed
packets of needles. These needles inside
have caused at first uneasiness and alarm for
the consequences ; but when they gradually,
and in succession, work out, some at the
elbows, some at the finger ends, some at the
nose, and in the end come all away, they
cease to trouble, and become a joke. It is

so with our moral transgressions. When committed, they plunge us in an agony of remorse and fear; but gradually they work out of us, point or head foremost, and finally we get rid of them altogether. Now Marianne Welsh and Stephen Saltren had swallowed a packet of needles between them, and they were all her needles which had entered him. She did not retain hers long, but as they worked out of her, they worked into him and transfixed his heart, which bristled with them, like a christening pin-cushion. This, of course, was particularly annoying to her. To forgive and to forget is a Christian virtue, and Saltren, she argued, was no better than a heathen, for all his profession, because he neither forgot nor forgave.

When Mrs. Saltren made the announcement to her brother and husband, that a cruel fraud had been committed on her, she had acted without premeditation, stung to the confession by her galled vanity at her brother's disrespectful tone, and with an indefined, immatured desire of setting herself to rights with her husband.

The story had been contemptuously cast back in her face by James Welsh; and it was with some surprise and much satisfaction, that she saw her husband ready to accept it without question. Captain Saltren had not offered to accompany his brother-in-law to the station, which was four miles distant; he could hardly wait with patience his departure. No sooner was Welsh gone, than Saltren grasped his wife's arm, and said in his deepest tones, " Tell me all, Marianne, tell me all ! "

" I ought," said Mrs. Saltren, recovering herself from the confusion which she felt, when her brother ridiculed her story, " I ought at this day to wear a coronet of diamonds. I was loved by a distinguished nobleman, with ardour. I cannot say that I loved him equally ; but I was dazzled. His family naturally were strenuously opposed to our union ; but, indeed, they knew nothing at all about it. He entreated me to consent to have our union celebrated in private. He undertook to obtain a special licence from the Archbishop. How was I to know that my simplicity was being imposed upon? I was an innocent, confiding girl, ignorant of the world's deceit; and extraordinarily good-looking."

"And you did not reckon on the wickedness of the aristocracy. Go on."

But Marianne paused. She was not ready to fill up the details, and to complete her narrative without consideration.

"Do not keep me in torture!" protested Saltren, his face was twitching convulsively

"How could I help myself?" asked Marianne. "It was not my fault that I had such an exquisite complexion, such abundant beautiful hair, and such lovely eyes; though, heaven knows, little did I know it then, or have I thought of, or valued it since. My beauty is, to some extent, gone now, but not altogether. As for my teeth, Stephen, which were pearls—I had not a decayed one in my jaws then; but after I married you they began to go with worry, and because you did not trust me, and were unkind to me!"

"Marianne," said Saltren, "you deceived

me—you deceived me cruelly. You told me nothing of this when I married you."

"I was always a woman of delicacy, and it was not for me to speak. I had been deceived and was deserted. Only when too late did I find how wickedly I had been betrayed, and then, when you came by and found me in my sorrow and desolation, I clung to your hand; I hoped you would be my consolation, my stay, my solace, and I— I——" She burst into tears. "I have been bitterly disappointed. I have found you without love, churlish, sullen, holding me from you as if I were infected with the plague, not ready to clasp me as an unhappy, suffering woman, that needed all the love and pity you could give."

"Not one word did you tell me of all this. You let me marry you in unsuspicion that before you had loved another."

"Not at all, Stephen," she said, "I have already assured you that I did not love the man whom I so foolishly and unfortunately trusted."

"Why have you not told me this story

long ago ? Why have you left me in the
dark so long ? "

" Your own fault, Stephen, none but yours.
If you had shown me that consideration
which becomes a professing Christian, I
might have been encouraged to open my
poor, tired, fluttering heart to you ; but I
was always a woman of extreme delicacy, and
very reserved. You, however, were distant,
and cold, and jealous. Then my pride bade
me keep my tragic story to myself."

Saltren stood before her with folded arms,
his hands were working. He could not keep
them still but by clasping them to his side.
" I was just, Marianne ! " he said. " Just,
and not severe to judge. I judged but as I
knew the facts. If I was told nothing, I
knew nothing to extenuate your fault. You
were young and beautiful, and I thought that
perhaps you had not strong principles to
guide you. Now that you have told me all,
I allow that you were more sinned against
than sinning ; but I cannot acquit you of not
entrusting me before this with the whole
truth."

" You never asked me for it."

" No," he answered sternly. " I could not do that. It was for you to have spoken."

Then, all at once, Saltren began to tremble; he took hold of the window-jamb, and he shook so that the diamond panes in the casement rattled. He stood there quivering in all his limbs. Great drops formed and rolled off his tall forehead, hung a moment suspended on his shaggy brow and then fell to the ground. They were not tears, they were the anguish drops expressed from his brain.

Mrs. Saltren looked at him with astonishment and some trepidation. She never had comprehended him. She could not understand what was going on in him now.

" What is it, Stephen ? "

He waved his hand. He could not speak.

" But, Stephen, what is it ? Are you ill ? "

Then he threw himself before her, and clasped her to him furiously, with a cry and a sob, and broke into a convulsion of loud weeping. He kissed her forehead, hair, and lips. He seized her hands, and covered them at once with tears and kisses.

"Marianne!" he said at last, with a voice interrupted and choked. "For all these years we have been divided, you and I, I and you, under one roof, and yet with the whole world between us. I never loved any but you—never, never any; and all these long years there has been my old love deep in my heart, not dead, but sleeping; and now and then putting up its hands and uttering a cry, and I have bid it go to sleep again and lie still, and never hoped that the trumpet would sound, and it would spring up to life once more. But why did you not tell me this before? Why did you hide from me that you were the sufferer, you the wronged? If you would have told me this, I would have forgiven you long ago. My heart has been hungering and crying out for love. I have seen you every day, and felt that I have loved you, felt it in every vein. To me you have not grown old, but have remained the same, only there was this shadow of a great darkness between us. I constrained myself, because I considered you had sinned against God and me, and were unworthy of being loved!"

Again he drew her head to his shoulder, laid it there, and kissed her, and sobbed, and clasped her passionately.

"Marianne! Let him that is without guilt cast the first stone. I forgive you. Tell me that you loved me when I came to you asking you to be mine."

"I did love you, Stephen—you and you only."

"And that other; he who—" he did not finish the sentence—a fresh fit of trembling came on him.

"I never did love him, Stephen. Only his title and his position impressed me. I was young, and he was so much my superior in age, in rank, in strength; and the prospect opened before me was so splendid, that a poor, young, trustful, foolish thing like me—"

"You did not love him?" Stephen spoke with eagerness.

"I have assured you that I never did."

"Oh the age that we have spent together under one roof, united yet separated ; one in name, apart in soul ; years of sorrow to both of us ; years of estrangement ; years of disappointed love, and broken trust, and em bittered home—all this we owe to him ! "

Marianne felt his heart beating furiously, and his muscles contracting spasmodically in his face, that was against hers, in his breast, in his arms.

Has it ever chanced to the reader to encounter a married couple blind to each other's faults, and these faults glaring ? One might suppose that daily intercourse would have sharpened the perception of each other's weaknesses, but instead of that it blunts it. They cannot detect in each other the grotesque, the ugly, the false, that are conspicuous and offensive to everyone else. Love, it is, which has softly dropped the veil over their eyes, or withdrawn from them the faculty of perceiving in each other these blemishes which, if perceived, would make common life unendurable. Love is well painted as blind, but the blindest of all loves is the love

of the married. In the case of the Saltrens
the blindness was on one side only, because
on his side only was there true love. This
had dulled his perception, so that he saw not
the shallowness, untruthfulness, vanity, and
heartlessness of Marianne, qualities which
her brother saw clearly enough.

"You have borne your wrong all these
years unavenged," he said. "My God! how
I have misjudged you! One word more,
Marianne." He disengaged himself from
her. He had been kneeling with his arms
enfolding her; now he released his hold, and
knelt, bolt-upright, with his hands depending
to the floor, gaunt, ungainly, motionless.
"Marianne," he said, slowly, "I know so
much that I must be told all. I must know
the rest." He paused for full a minute, looking her steadily in the face, still kneeling up-
right, stiffly, uncouthly. "Who was he?"

Marianne did not speak. Now in turn
agitation overcame her. Had she gone too
far with this story, true or false?

She raised her hands deprecatingly. What
would the consequences be?

Then, all at once, with a shriek rather than a cry, Saltren leaped to his feet.

"You need not say a word. I know all now, all—without your telling me. You were in the park at the time with the old Lady Lamerton, and—and you had the boy named after him."

Had there been light in the room, it would have been seen how pale was the face of Mrs. Saltren, but that of her husband, the captain, had turned a deadlier white still.

"It all unfolds before me, all becomes plain!" he cried. "I wondered whose was the head I saw on the book."

"On what book, Stephen?"

"I feared, I doubted, but now I doubt no more. It was his likeness!"

"What book do you mean?"

"The book of the Everlasting Gospel which I saw an angel carry in his right hand, flying in the midst of heaven; and he cast the book down, and the book was dipped in blood; and when it fell into the water, the water was turned to blood, as the river of Egypt when Israel was about to escape."

The door flew open, and Giles Inglett Saltren entered, wearing a light coat thrown over his evening dress. As he came in he removed his hat.

Captain Saltren turned on him with flashing eyes, and in his most sonorous tones said, as he waved him away : " Go back, go back whence you came. You have no part in me. You are not my son. Return to him who has cared for you : to him who is your father —Lord Lamerton."

CHAPTER XVII

HOW JINGLES TOOK IT.

GILES INGLETT SALTREN stood motionless, his hat in one hand, with the other holding the door, looking at the captain. No lamp had been lighted in the room since the sun had set, and he could only see his father's face indistinctly by the pale evening sky light cast in through window and door. But he would have known from the tones of his father's voice that he was profoundly moved, even if he had not caught the words he uttered. At first, indeed, he was too surprised to comprehend the full force of these words ; but, when their significance became clear to him, he also became moved, and he said gravely :

" This must be explained."

" What I said is quickly explained," answered the captain; and he rose to his feet.

Does the reader remember a familiar toy

of childhood composed of pretty birds, with feathers stuck in them, strung on horsehair or wires so as to form a sort of cage, but with this difference, that the cage did not contain the birds? When this toy was set down, all the little figures quivered slowly, uncertainly, to the bottom, and, when it was reversed, the same process was repeated. It was so with the captain's speech. His words were threaded on the tremulous strings of his vocal organ, and not only quivered from a high pitch down, but also went up from a low one with much vibration on high. A voice of this quality is provocative of sympathy; as, when a violoncello string is touched, a piano chord trembles responsive. Such voices make not the voices, but the hearts of other men to tremble. I know a slater who, when I am ordering of him slates, brings tears into my eyes by asking if I will have " Duchess " or " Rag."

" My words are quickly explained," said Stephen Saltren. " I have never regarded you as my son—have never treated you as such. You know that I have shown you no fatherly affection, because I knew from the beginning that not a drop of my blood flowed in your veins. But never, before this evening, have I allowed you, or any one else, to suspect what I knew, lest the honour of your mother should suffer. Now, and only now, has the entire truth been disclosed to me. I did not suspect it, no, not when you were christened and given the name you bear. I thought it was a compliment paid through a fancy of your mother's to the family in which she had lived, that was all. A little flickering suspicion may have been aroused afterwards, when his lordship, to save you from consumption, sent you abroad; but I put it angrily from me as unworthy of being harboured. I had no real grounds for suspicion; since then it has come up in my heart again and again, and I have stamped down the hateful thought with a kind of rage and shame at myself for thinking it. Only to-night has the whole story been told me, and I find that your mother was not to blame— that no real dishonour stains her—that all the fault, all the guilt, lies on and blackens— blackens and degrades his soul!"

" I did not mean to say—that is, I did not wish—" began Mrs. Saltren in a weeping, expostulating tone.

" Marianne, say nothing," Captain Saltren turned to her. " It is not for you to justify yourself to your child. The story shall be told him by me. I will spare you the pain and shame."

" But, mother," said Jingles, shutting the door behind him and leaning his back against it, " I must be told the whole truth. I must have it at least confirmed by your lips."

" My dear,"—Mrs. Saltren's voice shook —"I would not make mischief, for the world. I hate above everything the mischief-makers. If there be one kind of people I abhor it is those who make mischief ; and I am, thank heaven, not one of such."

" Quite so," said her son, gravely ; " but I must know what I have to believe, for I must act on it."

"Oh, my dear, do nothing! Let it remain, if you love me, just as if it had never been told. I should die of shame were it to come out."

"It shall not come out," said Giles ; "but I must know from your lips, mother, whether I am—I cannot say it. My happiness, my future depend on my knowledge of what my real parentage is. You can understand that?"

"Well, then, it is true that you are not Stephen Saltren's son, and it is true that I was a shamefully-used and deceived woman, and that I had no bad intentions whatever. I was always a person of remarkable delicacy and refinement above my station. As for who your father was, I name no names; and, indeed, just now, when the captain asked me, I said the same—that I would name no names, and so I stick to the same resolution, and nothing more shall be torn from me, not if you were to tear me to pieces with a chain harrow."

"Come without," said the captain, "and you shall hear from me how it came to pass. We must spare your mother's feelings. She was not in fault, she was wickedly imposed on."

Then the mining captain moved to the door ; Giles Inglett opened, and stood aside to allow his reputed father to go through; then he followed him and shut the door behind them.

Half an hour passed. Mrs. Saltren remained for some minutes seated where she had been, consoling herself with the reflection that she had named no names; and that, if mischief came of this, the fault would attach to Saltren, not to her. A little while ago we said that love was blind, hymeneal love most blind; but blind with incurable ophthalmia, blindest of all blindness, is self-love.

Mrs. Saltren rose and went about her domestic affairs.

"No one can charge me," said she, "with having kept my house untidy, or with having left unmended my husband's clothes. To think of the cartloads of buttons I've put on during my married life! It is enough to convince any but the envious. Well, it is a comfort that Stephen has been brought to his senses at last, and come to view matters in a proper light. I've heard James say that there is a nerve goes from each eyeball into the brain, and afore they enter it they take a twist about each other, and, so coupled, march in together. And James said if it were not so we should see double, and neither eye would agree with the other. I mind quite well that he said this one day when I was complaining to him that Stephen and I didn't get on quite right together. He said we'd get our twist one day and then see all alike. What he said is come true; leastways, the proper twist has come in Stephen. Thank God, I always see straight."

She went to a corner cupboard and opened it.

"Now that Stephen is gone," she said, "I'll rinse out the glass James had for his gin-and-water. Saltren is that crazy on teetotalism that he would be angry if he knew I had given James any, and angry to think I kept spirits in the house; and because he is so stupid I'm obliged to put it in a medicine-bottle with 'For outward application only' on it, and say it is a lotion for neuralgia. It is a mercy that I named no names, so my conscience is clear. It is just as in

Egypt, when there was darkness over all the land, the Israelites had light in their dwellings. I thank goodness I've always the clearest of light in me."

She removed the tumbler and washed it in the back kitchen.

"When one comes to consider it, after all, Stephen isn't so very much out in his reckoning. When does a nobleman take a delicate lad out of a school and send him to a warm climate because his lungs are affected, and then give him scholarship and college education, without having something that makes him do it? Are there no other delicate lads with weak lungs besides Giles? Why did not his lordship send them to Bordighera? Are there no other clever young fellows in national schools besides my boy, to be taken up and pushed on? There must have been some reason for my lord selecting Giles. Was it because I had been in service in the house? Other young women out of the park have married and had children, but I never heard of my lord doing anything for their sons. None of

them have been sent to college and made
into gentlemen except my boy. But then I
was uncommonly good-looking, that is true,
and not another young hussey at the park
was fit to hold a candle to me. Though, the
Lord knows, I never set store on good looks.
If it pleases his lordship to treat Giles almost
as if he were a son, he has a right to do so,
but he must take the consequences. I don't
interfere with the fancies of others, but if any
one chooses to do a queer thing, he must
expect to have to answer for it. I have no
doubt that his lordship has frequently wished
he had a son, such a fine and handsome
fellow as my Giles, and for some years he
was without any son of his own to inherit his
title. There was only Miss Arminell.
Anyhow, no responsibility attaches to me,
whatever may be said. No one can blame
me. His lordship ought never to have taken
notice of Giles, never to have had the doctor
examine his lungs, and, when told that the
boy would die unless sent to the south of
France, he should have said, ' He is the son
of poor parents, who can't afford the expense,

so I suppose he must die.' No one could have blamed him, then. And when Giles came back—better, but still delicate, and not suited to do hard work—my lord should not have sent him to school and college, and taken him in at Orleigh Park as tutor to his son—he should not have done any of these things unless he had made up his mind to take the consequences. Scripture says that no man sets down to build a tower without having first counted the cost. It is not at all unlikely that folks will say queer things, and I know for certain my husband thinks queer fancies about my boy and Lord Lamerton ; but who is to blame for that? If his lordship didn't want to make it thought by all the world that Giles was his son, all I can say is, he shouldn't have done for him what he did. It is not my place to stop idle talk. I'd like to know whether it is any woman's duty to run about a parish correcting the mistakes made by the gossiping tongues therein. I thank heaven I am not a gadabout. I do my duty, washing, and ironing, and mending of waistcoats, and sewing on of buttons, and

darning of stocking-feet, and baking of meat-
dumplings, and peeling of potatoes ; that is
what my work is, and I do it well.   I don't
take upon me the putting to rights of other
folks when in error.   Every one stands for
himself.   If you cut the wick crooked you
must expect your chimney-glass to get
smoked, and, if Lord Lamerton has snipped
his wick askew, he must look out for fish-
tails."

Mrs. Saltren removed her petroleum lamp-
glass, struck a match, and proceeded slowly
to light her lamp.

" I remember James telling me once, how
that he had been in France, I think he called
it La Vendée, where the fields are divided
by dykes full of stagnant water ; and one of
the industries of the place is the collecting of
leeches.   The men roll up their breeches
above the knee and carry a pail, and wade in
the ditches, and now and again throw up a
leg, and sweep off two, three, or it may be a
dozen leeches from the calf into the pail.
Then they wade further, and up with a leg
again and off with a fresh batch of leeches.

I haven't been in a big house, and seen the
ways of the aristocracy, and not found out
that they are waders in leech dykes, and that
it is as much as they can do to keep their
calves clear, and their blood from being
sucked out of them altogether. Now what I
want to know is, if a starved leech does bite,
and suck and swell, and is not wiped off and
sent to market, but gets reg'lar blown out
with blood, hasn't that leech a right to say
that he has in him the blood of the man to
whom he has attached himself? I'd ask any
independent jury whether my Giles Inglett
has eaten and drunk more at Saltren's expense, or at that of his lordship, whether he
does not owe his very life to his lordship as
much as to me, for he'd have died of decline,
if he had not been sent to the South? And
if he owes his life to Lord Lamerton equally
as he does to me, and has been fed and
clothed, and educated by him and not by
Saltren, why then, like the leech, he can say
he has the blood of the Lamertons in him.
That is common sense. And again—bother
that lamp!"

Mrs. Saltren in place of turning the wick up, had turned it down, and was obliged to remove the chimney and strike another match.

"And then," she continued, "if Lord Lamerton has not chose to wipe him off into the pail, who is to blame but himself? If he choose to keep his leg in a leech pond, there's neither rhyme nor reason in my objecting; and he has no claim to cry out. Put Giles on a plate, and sprinkle salt on him, and whose blood will come out? Any one can see he is a gentleman! He has imbibed it all, his manners, his polish, his knowledge, everything he has, from Lord Lamerton and others, all the world can see it."

Then in came the young man about whom she was arguing with herself. He could not speak, so great was his agitation, but he went to his mother, and threw his arms about her, clasped her to his heart, and kissed her. For some time he could not say anything, but after a while he conquered his emotion sufficiently to say—

" Oh, my mother—my poor mother! Oh,

my dear, my ill-used mother!" and then again his emotions got the better of him. "I cannot," he said, after a pause, with a renewed effort to govern himself, "I cannot say what I shall do now, I cannot even think, but I am sure of one thing, I must remain no longer at the park."

"My boy!" exclaimed Mrs. Saltren. "Fall off yourself into the plate and salt!"

"I do not understand," said he. She left him in his ignorance, she had been thinking of the leeches.

"My dear Giles! Whatever you do, don't breathe a word of this to any one."

"Mother, I will not, you may be sure of that."

"Not to Lord Lamerton above all—not for heaven's sake."

"Least of all to him."

' I should get into such trouble. Oh, my gracious!"

"Mother, dear," the young fellow clasped her to his heart again—"how inexpressibly precious you are to me now, and how I grieve for you. I can say no more now."

Then he went forth.

"Why, bless me!" exclaimed Mrs. Saltren. "He never was so affectionate before. Well, as far as human reason goes, it does seem as if all things were being brought to their best for me; for this day has given me my husband's love and doubled that of my son."

Giles Inglett Saltren walked hastily back to the park. On his way he encountered Samuel Ceely, who put forth his maimed hand, and crooked the remaining fingers in his overcoat, to arrest him, as he went by.

"What do you want with me?" asked Jingles impatiently.

" I should be so glad if you would put in a word for me," pleaded the old man.

" I am engaged—I cannot wait."

" But," urged old Ceely, without letting go his hold, " Joan has axed Miss Arminell for a scullery-maid's place for me. Now I'd rather have to do wi' the dogs, or I could keep the guns beautifully clean, or even the stables."

" I really cannot attend to this!" said

Jingles, impatiently. " I have other matters of more importance now on my mind ; besides, my influence is not what—" he spoke bitterly—"what it should be in the great house."

"You might do me a good turn, and speak a word for me."

" The probability of my speaking a good word for you, or any one to Lord Lamerton, or of doing any one a good turn in Orleigh Park, is gone from me for ever," said Giles. " You must detain me no longer—it is useless. Let me go."

He shook himself free from the clutch of the old man, and walked along the road.

After he had gone several paces, perhaps a hundred yards, he turned—moved by what impulse was unknown to him—and looked back. In the road, lit by the moon, stood the cripple, stretching forth his maimed hand after him, with the claw-like fingers.

CHAPTER XVIII.

HOW ARMINELL TOOK IT.

GILES INGLETT SALTREN walked on fast, he was disturbed in the stream of his thoughts by the interruption of the tiresome old cripple. He had more important matters to occupy his mind than the requirements of Samuel Ceely. His heart beat, his hands became moist. What a marvellous disclosure had been made to him—and he wondered at himself for not having divined it before. He argued much as did his mother. Why had Lord Lamerton done such great things for him, why had he sent him abroad, found him money, given him education, lifted him far above the sphere in which his parents moved, unless he felt called to do so by a sense of responsibility, such as belongs to a father?

To a whole class of minds disinterested conduct is inconceivable. All such conduct as is oblique is to them intelligible, and

allowance is made by them for stupidity,
and stupidity with them is the same thing as
unselfishness. But such unselfishness is
permissible only by fits as lapses from the
course which all men naturally take. But
that men should act consistently on disinterested motives is an idea too preposterous
for them to allow of its existence.

This class of minds does not belong
specially to any particular stratum of society,
though it is found to be most prevalent
where the struggle for existence is most
keen, and where there is least culture.

But of culture there are two kinds, that
which is external, and that which is within ;
it is generally found that this inability to
understand disinterested conduct is found
everywhere where the inner culture does
not exist.

There is, we believe, a Rabbinic legend
concerning a certain cow which was its own
calf, and much disputation ensued among
the Talmudists, to determine the point of
time at which the cow calved itself, and when
it ceased to be accounted beef, and became

veal, or the contrary. But what seems to us Gentiles to be impossible in the material sense, is possible enough in the spiritual realm, and a very calf-like self may become the mother of a cow-self, so vast, so considerable that, like the Brahminic cow, Varuna, it will occupy the entire firmament, extend to the horizon on all sides, and overshadow and envelope everything. Varuna in fact is the universe, and as we see and exist in that universe, so with the cow-self born of calf-self, it becomes our universe. We see only that cow, inhale the breath of that cow, think only cow thoughts, stand on cow, and our aspirations are limited on all sides by cow. That cow is Self born of self. The breath of that cow is sweet to our nostrils, its milk the nourishment of our bowels, its low is music to our ears, and nothing that does not smell and taste and sound of that cow is worthy of being smelt, and tasted, and listened to.

Of this cow we can give information unattainable by the Rabbis. We can watch its development, if we cannot determine the

moment of its nativity. It probably comes
to the birth at an early age, but there is this
deserving of consideration about it that this
cow born of calf can be bled to whiteness,
and knocked on the head if taken in time.

If, however, it be allowed to attain to
heiferhood, it is thenceforth unmanageable;
we see everything through its medium, and
like and dislike, love and hate all objects and
persons as they stand within or without of
the compass of the great cow-self, which has
become our Varuna, our universe.

It must not be supposed that such as live
under the shadow of this great cow, are op-
pressed by it. On the contrary they have
become so accustomed to it that they could
not exist apart from it. There is a story of
a man who carried a monstrous cow on his
shoulders, and explained that he had acquired the ability to do so by beginning
with the creature when it was a day old. As
the calf grew, so grew his ability to support
its weight. It is the same with us, we
carry the little calf-self about on our shoulder,
and dance along the road and leap over the

stones, and as day by day the calf grows, so does our capacity for carrying it, till at last we trudge about everywhere, into all society, even into church, with the monstrous cow-self on our shoulders, and do not feel that we have anything weighing on us whatsoever.

Now Giles Inglett Saltren had grown up nursing and petting this calf. He had good natural abilities, but partly through his mother's folly, partly through external circumstances, he had come to see everything through a medium of self. The notice taken of him by his schoolmaster because he was intelligent, by Lord Lamerton because he was delicate, the very stethoscoping of his lungs, the jellies and grapes sent him from the great house, the petting he got in the servants' hall, because he was handsome and interesting, the superiority he had acquired over his parents by his residence abroad, and education, all tended to the feeding and fattening of the calf-self; and the cod-liver oil he had consumed, had not merely gone to restore his lungs, but to build up piles of yellow fat on the flanks of self. Jingles had already reached that point at which his cow had become Varuna, his entire universe. He thought of, considered, nothing from any other point of view than as it touched himself.

His consciousness of discomfort in the society at Orleigh, his bitterness of mood, his resentment of the distinctions not purposely made, but naturally existing and necessarily insuperable, between himself and those with whom he associated, all this sprang out of the one source, all came of the one disease—intense, all-absorbing, all prevailing selfishness.

He observed the natural ease that pervaded all the actions of those with whom he was brought into contact in the upper world, and their complete lack of self-consciousness, their naturalness, simplicity, in all they said and did. He had not got it—he could not acquire it, he was like a maid-of-all work from a farmhouse on a market day in the county town wearing a Mephistopheles hat on her red head, and ten-button gloves on her mottled arms. He was conscious of his self-consciousness—he feared it would be remarked. It made him suspicious and envious and angry. He could not reach to the ease of those above him, and therefore he desired to level them to his own plane. A man with black blood in his veins is fearful lest those at the table should look at his nails. Jingles was ever dreading lest some chance glance should discover the want of breed in himself.

This caused him much misery; and this all came of his carrying about the cow-self with him into my lady's boudoir, and my lord's study, to the dining-room, and to the parlour.

I was at the autumn fair some years ago at Liège; on the boulevards were streets of booths, some for the sale of cakes and toys, others shows; but, as among the stalls those for cakes prevailed, so among the shows did the Rigolade Parisienne preponderate.

Not having the faintest conception of what the Rigolade was, I paid my sou and entered one in quest of knowledge; and this is what I saw—a series of mirrors. But there was this peculiar about the mirrors, one was convex, and in it I beheld my nose reduced to a pimple, and my eyes to currants ; another was concave, in which my nose swelled to a proboscis and my eyes to plums. A third mirror multiplied my face fifty times. A fourth showed me my face elongated, as when my MS. has been returned "not suited," from an editor ; a fifth widened my face to an absurd grin ; in a sixth I saw my pleasant self magnified in serene and smiling beauty in the midst, and showed me every surrounding person and object, the faces of men, the houses, the cathedral, the sky, the sun, all distorted out of shape and proportions. " Eh ça, M'sou," said the showman, "c'est la véritable Rigolade Parisienne."

Eh ça—my dear readers, was Giles Inglett Saltren's vision of life. He saw himself, infinitely magnified, and everything else dwarfed about him and tortured into monstrosity.

Of one thing I am very certain, dear reader, in this great Rigolade of life into which we have entered, and through which we are walking, there are some who are always seeing themselves in the multiplying mirror, and there are others who contemplate their faces continually elongated, whilst others again see themselves in the widening mirror and accommodate themselves to be the perpetual buffoon. Let us trust that these are not many, but there certainly are some who view themselves enlarged, and view everything and every person beside, the world about them, the heaven above them, in a state of distortion.

Lord Lamerton had shown the young tutor extraordinary kindness, for he was a man with a soft heart, and he really wished to make the young fellow happy. He would have liked Giles to have opened out to him and not to have maintained a formal distance, but he was unable to do more than invite confidence, and he attributed the stiffness of the tutor to his shyness. Of late, his lordship had begun to think that perhaps Jingles was somewhat morbid, but this he attributed to his constitutional delicacy. Consumptive people are fantastical, was his hasty generalization.

In the heart of Giles Inglett Saltren a very mixed feeling existed as he walked back to the park. He was gratified to think that he had noble blood in his veins, but he was incensed at the thought of the treachery to which his mother had fallen a vict m, and which robbed him of his birth-rights. Had that function in the drawing-room, described by his mother, been cele-brated legally, he and not the snivelling little Giles would be heir to Orleigh, to fifty thou and a year, and a coronet, and a seat in the House of Lords. What use would Giles the Little make of his privileges? Would he not lead the same prosaic life as his fathe , planting pines, digging fish-ponds, keeping a pack of hounds, doing the active work of a county magnate and magistrate—whereas he—Giles Inglett Saltren, no longer Saltren, but Baron Lamerton of Orleigh, might become, with the advantages of his birth, wealth, and abilities combined, the greatest statesman and reformer England had known. He felt that his head was bursting with ideas, his blood on fire to give them utterance, and his hands tingling to carry his projects into effect. Without some adventitious help, such as position and wealth could give, he could not take the place he knew by inner illumination should be his.

" I was sure of it," said Jingles, " that is to say I imagined that I could not be the son of a common mining captain. There was something superior to that sort of stuff in me. But now this infamous act of treachery stands between me and acknowledgment by the world, between me and such success as, perhaps no man in England, except perhaps Mr. Gladstone, has attained to. All I want is a lift on the ladder—after that first step I will mount the rest of the way myself."

He walked on fast. His blood seethed in his heart. He was angry with Lord Lamerton for having betrayed his mother's trust, and with his mother for allowing herself to be deceived.

" Something may yet be done. It is not impossible that I may discover what has not been suspected. I must discover this friend who pretended to be a parson, and search the archiepiscopal registers for the alleged licence. It is hardly likely, that my lord would dare to fabricate a false licence, or for a friend of his to run the risk, out of friendship, of twenty-five years' penal servitude. No—it is, calmly considered, far more likely that a true licence was obtained, that the marriage though secret, was valid, and that my mother was imposed upon, when assured she had been duped, and then she was forced on Captain Saltren to dispose of her securely against discovering her rights and demanding them. I will go to town and then take advice what to do. It will, perhaps, be best for me thence to write to his lordship and ask for the particulars, threatening unless they are furnished me voluntarily, that I will search them out for myself. If I were the Honourable Giles Inglett," mused Jingles, with his eyes on the moonlit road, " how utterly different my position in the house would be to what it now is. That confounded butler—who assumes a patronising air, and would, if I gave him encouragement, pat me on the shoulder. That impudent valet, who brought me up the wrong waist-coat yesterday morning and allowed me to ring thrice before he chose to answer the bell, and never apologised for having kept me waiting. Then, again, at table the other day, when something was said of fish out of water, the footman touched my back with the dish of curried prawns. He did it intentionally, he meant that I was a fish out of water, a curried prawn myself, in fiery heat. There was something said among the gentlemen about Gammon, the man who has just been created High Sheriff. He made his money in mines. One of those present said that those fellows who scramble into society for which they are not qualified always reminded him of French poodles, half-shaven and half-savage; every one laughed and the laugh cut me like knives. I am sure several at the table thought of me, and that they have taken to calling to me 'the French poodle.' What am I? I am either his lordship's legitimate but unacknowledged son—and if so I am shaved all over: but if I am as he would pretend, his bastard—I am half-shaved, and so half-shaved I must run about the world, laughed at, thought monstrous, pitied, a creature of aristocratic and plebeian origin commingled, with the hair about my neck, and ears, and eyes, and nose, but all the rest of me polished and cultured. A poodle indeed ! I—a French poodle ! "

A piece of decayed branch fallen from a tree lay in the road. Jingles kicked it away.

" That," said he passionately, " is what I should like to do to the butler, were I the Honourable Giles. And that," he kicked another stick, " is how I would treat that brute who allowed me to wait for my waistcoat. And so," he trod on and snapped a twig that lay athwart his path, " so would I crush the footman who dared to nudge me with the curried prawns ! And," he caught a hazel bough that hung from the hedge, and broke it off, and ripped the leaves away, and then with his teeth pulled the rind away, " and this is what I would do to that man who dared to talk of half-shaved French poodles. Oh ! if I could be but a despot—a dictator for an hour—for an hour only—to ram the curried prawns down the throat of that insolent ruffian who nudged me, and to flay alive that creature who spoke of poodles! Then I would cheerfully surrender my power into the hands of the people and be the democratic leader once more."

He entered the park grounds by a side-gate and was soon on the terrace. There he saw Arminell returning to the house from her stroll in the avenue.

" Mr. Saltren," she said, " have you also been enjoying the beauty of the night ? "

" I have been trying to cool the fever within," he replied.

" I hope," she said, misunderstanding him, "that you have not caught the influenza, or whatever it is from Giles."

" I have taken nothing from Giles. The fever I speak of is not physical."

" Oh ! you are still thinking of what we discussed over the Noah's Ark."

" Yes—how can I help it ? I who am broken and trodden on at every moment."

" I am sorry to hear you say this, Mr.

Saltren. I also have been talking the matter
over with papa, and after he went in, I have
been walking up and down under the trees
meditating on it—but I get no farther, for all
my thinking."

"Miss Inglett," said Jingles, "the time of
barley-mows is at an end. Hitherto we have
had the oats, and the wheat, and the rye,
and the clover, and the meadow-grass ricked,
stacked separately. All that is of the past.
The age of the stack-yard is over with its
several distinct classified ricks—this is wheat,
that is rye ; this is clover, that damaged hay.
We are now entering an age of Silo, and inevitably as feudalism is done away with, so
will the last relics of distinctions be swept
aside also, and we shall all enter an universal
and common silo."

"I do not think I quite understand you."

"Henceforth all mankind will make one,
all contribute to the common good, all be
pressed together and the individuality of one
pass to become the property of all."

Arminell shook her head and laughed.

"I confess that I find great sweetness in

the old stack-yard, and a special fragrance attaches to each rick. Is all that to be a thing of the past, and the savour of the silo to be the social atmosphere of the future?"

"You strain the illustration," said Saltren testily.

"You wish to substitute an aggregate of nastiness for diversified sweets."

"Miss Inglett, I will say no more. I thought you more sympathetic with the aspirations of the despised and down-trodden, with the movement of ideas in the present century."

"I am sympathetic," said Arminell. "But I am as bewildered now as I was this morning. I am just as one who has been spun through the spiral tunnel on the St. Gothard line, when one rushes forth into day ; you know neither in which direction you are going, nor to what level you are brought. I dislike your similitude of a silo, and so have a right to criticise it."

"Arminell," said Jingles, standing still.

"Mr. Saltren!" The girl reared herself haughtily, and spoke with icy coldness.

"Exactly," laughed the tutor, bitterly. "I thought as much! You will not allow the presumed son of a manganese captain, the humble tutor, to presume an approach of familiarity to the honourable the daughter of a peer."

"I allow no one to presume," said she, haughtily, and turned her back on him, and resumed her walk.

"Yet I have a right," pursued Jingles, striding after her. "Miss Inglett—Arminell listen to me. I am not the man to presume. I know and am made to feel too sharply my inferiority to desire to take a liberty. But I have a right, and I stand on my right. I have a right to call you by your Christian name, a right which you will acknowledge. I am your brother."

Arminell halted, turned and looked at him from head to foot with surprise mingled with disdain.

"You doubt my words," he went on. "I am not offended—I am not surprised at that : indeed, I expected it. But what I say is true. We have different mothers, mine "—

u

with bitterness—" of the people, that I allow
— of the people, of the common, base lot,
who are dirt under your feet ; yours is of the
aristocracy, made much of, received in society,
in the magic circle from which mine would
be shut out. But we have one father ; I
stand to you in precisely the same relation as
does the boy Giles, but I am your elder
brother, and should be your adviser and
closest friend."

END OF VOLUME I.